DEATH
HAS A WILL

By

Amelia Reynolds Long

WILDSIDE PRESS

www.wildsidepress.com

1

TESTAMENT

(Tuesday, 2 p.m. to 2:30 p.m.)

I.

Old Mrs. Marsden surveyed the young man whom the nurse had just shown into her sitting room. She didn't do it through a lorgnette, but the effect was the same. Her gazed moved leisurely from the top of his dark head, lingered a moment upon the faint suggestion of sideburns that emphasized the lean curve of his cheek, then continued on down his slight figure to the tips of his immaculate white oxfords. Finally she remarked with a crispness unexpected in one so apparently frail:

"So you're Jeff Carter's younger brother. You don't look much like him."

The young man smiled engagingly.

"No, ma'am," he admitted; "I don't guess I do."

"Are you as good a lawyer as Jeff?"

"Oh, yes, ma'am. I'm better."

The old lady chuckled.

"I believe you are, at that," she said. "Anyway, you've got self-confidence, and that's what I want in a lawyer. You're from the South, aren't you?"

"Yes, ma'am; South Car'lina."

"I knew it as soon as you opened your mouth. What's your name? Your given name, I mean."

"Stephen."

"I think I'll call you that, keep you separate in my mind from Jeff. Sit down." She pointed with her gold-headed cane to a chair beside one of the open windows, through which could be heard the drone of bees among the splashes of red and white phlox in the garden below.

Stephen sat down obediently. He generally got on rather well with old ladies, particularly if they were what he called "a little sassy," and he decided that he was going to like this one. He placed his brief-case on the floor beside his chair, and waited for her to continue. After a moment she did.

"Your brother Jeff drew my husband's will five years ago," she

3

stated with the abruptness that Stephen was beginning to realize was characteristic of her. "But since he's become district attorney, he claims he can't draw mine. Of course, I could have gotten my grand-daughter, Veronica, to do it; she's a lawyer. But there are reasons why I'd rather not."

"Yes, ma'am; I understand."

"No, you don't either," she contradicted him. "You think I intend to leave Ronnie my money, but I don't. I'm leaving it to somebody that's not even a relation."

This time Stephen didn't venture a comment. He learned fast in such matters.

The old lady noted this, and approved.

"I'll tell you all about it in a minute," she went on. "But first, I want to know something: Can a will made by a—a crazy person be broken?"

Stephen considered.

"Well, now, that all depends," he answered carefully.

"On how crazy the person is?"

"No, ma'am, not exactly. More often it depends on how crazy the will is."

"Like leaving one's money to an outsider, for instance?"

"Not unless undue influence can be proven," Stephen replied. "Generally, the courts recognize that a person has the right to dispose of his property and money as he sees fit, especially if he's had the foresight to include a small legacy for any of the relatives that may attempt to contest the will. But, Mrs. Marsden, you're not crazy," he added, unable to hold the words back any longer.

She smiled grimly.

"Thank you, Stephen," she said. "I was beginning to have some doubts about that myself."

A singular expression, that Stephen found himself unable to interpret, flitted across her aristocratic old face; then almost immediately it was gone as she turned her head and glanced out of the window to where a man and a girl could be seen playing tennis on a grass court just beyond the garden. The girl was lithe and tanned, with close-cropped, dark hair that made her look engagingly like a young boy. The man was tall and wiry, with an air about him suggestive of a life spent in the open; yet this air was oddly belied by the peculiar pallor of his complexion. His expression was reserved, almost austere; then suddenly it changed completely as he smiled in response to some remark of the girl's.

Mrs. Marsden smiled too, as if in sympathy.

"You see that young man?" she said to Stephen. "His name is Whitney Hamilton. The girl with him is my granddaughter, Veronica, who is spending her vacation with me this summer. Those two are in love with each other, although neither one will admit it. Ronnie won't of course, because she's a woman; and even in this day and age, women have some pride left—at least, Marsden women do. And Whitney won't speak because—well, for fear of being considered a fortune hunter, for one thing. That's why I'm leaving my money to him instead of to Ronnie or my grandson, Ralph, who is already provided for in my late husband's will."

Stephen looked with new interest at the man down on the tennis court. There was something vaguely familiar about him, although, at the moment, Stephen could not have said what it was.

"Mr. Hamilton is a neighbor?" he inquired, hoping that the old lady's answer would provide the necessary jog to his memory. But he was to be disappointed.

"No, he isn't," she said shortly; then she added, "That is, he's only boarding with the Heisy girls next door." She gave her crisp little chuckle again. "They still call themselves the Heisy *girls*," she went on, "although Maime Heisy must be nearly seventy, and Phoebe is almost as old. But time stopped moving for them somewhere around the turn of the century; and if things aren't done the way 'our mom and our pap' used to do them, they're all wrong. 'Our pap,' by the way, was a banker who could take care of everybody's money except his own. That's why the girls have to keep what they call 'a paying guest.' "

Stephen smiled, but he wasn't at all deceived by this rather transparent effort to change the subject of conversation. It meant that he wasn't to ask too many questions about Whitney Hamilton. He wondered why.

"Now about the will," Mrs. Marsden went on. She clasped her thin, blue-veined hands about the knob of her cane. "I want to leave all my possessions, real and personal, to Whitney Hamilton; with the exception of one thousand dollars, which I leave to my grandson, Ralph Marsden. That ought to be enough to hold him, don't you think?"

Stephen nodded, and made a note of the conditions of the will he was to draw up. He wondered whether the old lady realized what a revealing sidelight upon the character of her grandson that last remark had been. Then another thought occurred to him.

."Mrs Marsden," he began, "I don't guess you want Miss Ronnie and Mr. Hamilton to have to wait until you're dead to get married. But if you tell him you're leaving him your money to smooth the way for him, he's still going to feel like a fortune hunter and a fool besides. Any decent man would."

Her bright old eyes clouded.

"I hadn't thought of that," she admitted. "This arranging of other people's lives for them isn't going to be as easy as I thought."

Stephen privately agreed with her. Aloud he asked:

"You're sure Mr. Hamilton would ask Miss Ronnie to marry him if it weren't for the money?"

She nodded, her gaze once more upon the tennis players.

"Yes," she answered. "He practically admitted as much to Phoebe Heisy."

"Then," Stephen said, "the thing for you to do is to let him know, not that he is to be your heir, but that Miss Ronnie isn't." Although he didn't add it, he thought that this would also serve another purpose in case, contrary to Mrs. Marsden's belief, Mr. Whitney Hamilton was a fortune hunter after all.

She brought her eyes back to his face. She was smiling now.

"You have got more brains than your brother!" she exclaimed. "Jeff would never have thought of that. I'll do it, but you'll have to help me."

She leaned slightly forward in her chair. There was an expression of sly devilment in her old eyes.

"I want you to go next door and call upon the Heisy's," she announced. "They're hiding behind the lace curtains at their dining room windows, watching you through their opera glasses, at this very minute. Tell them I've asked you to draw up a rather peculiar will, disinheriting my own relatives in favor of a stranger; and you want to know whether I'm—well, a little batty, as my grandson Ralph would say. Oh, I know that wouldn't be considered very ethical conduct for a lawyer ordinarily," she hurried on as she saw that he was about to protest, "but the Heisys won't know the difference. And Maime Heisy is better than a broadcasting station; whatever goes in her ears comes out her mouth in the shortest possible time. That way, Whitney will find out what I want him to know without the information seeming to come from me."

Before Stephen could answer, the nurse who had admitted him came into the room. She was a young woman, not bad to look at, with an air of self-confidence about her that added to her professional manner without being a part of it. She examined Stephen with a gaze that lingered just a second too long to be disinterestedly impersonal before she turned to her patient.

"I'm afraid you're going to tire yourself, Mrs. Marsden," she said. Her tone was solicitous, but not professionally wheedling. "Remember what Dr. Richards told you."

The old lady made a gesture of impatience.

"I'm all right, Helen," she answered. "I wish you and Dr. Richards would stop coddling me. One would think—"

She didn't finish the sentence. The nurse lingered for an instant in the doorway, then withdrew.

Stephen rose.

"I'll have the will ready for you to sign in the morning, Mrs. Marsden," he said.

He started to move toward the door when she stopped him.

"Wait a minute," she commanded. "There's something else."

She hesitated, while her eyes brooded upon her hands that still were clasped tightly about the gold knob of her cane. Then abruptly her manner changed.

"Never mind," she said. "We'll discuss that *after* I've signed the will."

II.

Miss Phoebe Heisy nudged her sister's elbow.

"Let me have the glasses now, Maime," she pleaded. "It's my turn."

Miss Maime did not lower the opera glasses from her eyes.

"Be still, Phoebe," she commanded. "You'll jog the curtain."

"Yes, ma'am?"

Miss Phoebe moved back a trifle so that she did not touch the stiff lace curtains that hung from the top of the window to the floor.

"What do you see now?" she asked.

"They're both looking out of the window," Miss Maime reported without turning her head. "They're watching Whitney and Ronnie. Now Mary Marsden is saying something, but I can't make out what it is."

"Let me look," Miss Phoebe pleaded again. "I'm better at lip reading than you are."

Miss Maime paid no attention.

"Now he's writing something in a notebook," she went on as though her sister had not spoken. "Phoebe, I'd give anything to know what Mary Marsden can be doing with a detective in her house.

"A detective? I thought Mr. Carter was a lawyer."

"So he is," impatiently; "but he's a sort of detective, too. Don't you remember the Raymond case?"

Miss Phoebe shivered deliciously. Detective mysteries, real and fictitious, were her secret vice. Miss Maime never bothered with them; they'd have been a busman's holiday for her.

Then of a sudden Miss Phoebe's face clouded.

"Maime!" she gasped apprehensively, while her hand moved in a little fluttery gesture in the general direction of her heart. "You don't suppose she—she's telling him about—Whitney?"

"Of course not," Miss Maime snapped, as though to settle the matter with the very force of her denial. "You think of the most outlandish things, Phoebe! And anyway, what is there to tell? Only that he was—"

"Don't say it!" Miss Phoebe interrupted fearfully. "Remember, we aren't supposed to know that."

Miss Maime was looking out of the window again.

"Mr. Carter's leaving now," she reported. "And Whitney and Ronnie have finished their tennis game. He's coming home now— Whitney, I mean. Remember, Phoebe: not a word about this to him."

A minute or so later the door from the side porch opened, and Whitney Hamilton came into the room. He crossed to where the two old ladies were standing and put an arm about the shoulders of each.

"What's so interesting out there, girls?" he inquired, one of his rare smiles transfiguring his face. "Been watching Ronnie and me play tennis? . . . No, you haven't either," as he caught sight of the opera glasses which Miss Maime was ineffectually trying to hide in a fold of her skirt. "You've been peeking at Mrs. Marsden again. Maime, I'm ashamed of you!"

Miss Maime bridled.

"No such thing!" she denied indignantly. "We've been studying the birds. Haven't we, Phoebe?"

"I don't know," Miss Phoebe said undiplomatically. "You wouldn't let me have the glasses."

Whitney laughed.

"All right, then," he agreed. "Birds it is. Who am I to doubt the word of my two best girls?"

"Oh, go along with you!" Miss Maime said airily.

He patted her shoulder, kissed Miss Phoebe lightly upon the cheek, then, picking up the tennis racket which he had laid across the seat of a chair when he came in, continued on to his own room.

"He's a nice boy," Miss Maime said when the door had closed behind him. "And he's going to be a fine man—just like our pap." It was the highest compliment she knew how to bestow.

"Yes," Miss Phoebe said almost fiercely. She was watching Stephen Carter get into his waiting automobile and drive away.

2

CONSPIRACY

(Tuesday, 3 p.m to 7:30 p.m.)

I.

Nurse Helen Godwin stood upon the side porch of the Marsden house, fanning herself absently with her handkerchief. Now that her patient was asleep, she had an hour or so free time; an hour or so in which to be alone, and to think.

Her bold brown eyes moved with an almost devouring look across the heat-shimmering garden past the gay-colored flowers of the perennial border surrounding the house itself, across the velvety green expanse of well kept lawn to the tree-shaded tennis court beyond. A place like this stood for something: security, wealth, position. She wondered whether the old lady asleep upstairs ever thought of these things. Probably not; those who had them generally took them for granted. Helen wondered whether, if she were mistress of such a place, she would come to feel that way, too. She toyed for a moment with the thought.

Then her mind moved to other matters. The young man who had called at the house less than an hour before was a lawyer. But Ronnie also was a lawyer; what did Mrs. Marsden want with another one? Did that mean—her hand suddenly stopped its monotonous, fan-like motion with the handkerchief—did that mean that Ronnie, and not Ralph—

A car turned in at the drive, interrupting her thoughts. It drew to a stop in front of the porch steps, and a man got out.

He was a little man, with a shining bald head, round, slightly bulging eyes and a pink, chubby face. On his chin he wore a close-clipped black Van Dyke, which gave him the ridiculous aspect of a baby that had begun miraculously to grow a beard. He turned to lift a physician's medical bag from the car; then he came up the steps to where Helen was standing.

"Good afternoon, Nurse." His voice was an unexpectedly deep bass.

"Good afternoon, Dr. Richards."

"Patient asleep?"

"Yes, Doctor."

He paused beside her, resting his medical case upon the porch railing in front of him.

"How does she seem today?"

"Quite bright and lively. Today has been one of her good days."

"No more talk of—hallucinations?"

Helen hesitated the barest instant; then:

"None that I know of," she answered.

He frowned at the large tiger's-eye ring on the middle finger of his left hand.

"None that you know of?" he repeated. "Exactly what does that mean, please?"

"Exactly what it seems to. She hasn't mentioned the—the hallucinations to me since the last time I told you about."

His frown deepened until his face had taken on the puckered aspect of a baby's that is about to cry.

"Miss Godwin," he began severely, "I can't say that I entirely approve of your conduct of this case. It seems to me that you are spending not enough time with your patient, and entirely too much of it with—shall we say, other members of the family?"

Her shoulders stiffened ever so slightly under her startched white uniform.

"Just what do you mean by that, Doctor?" she demanded.

"I think we understand each other." His round eyes had left the ring and were staring hard at her, as though they would bore their way through the professional formality which she had erected like a barrier between them. "Ralph Marsden, while he may not be a particularly attractive young man personally, stands to come into a sizeable amount of money under the terms of his late grandfather's will—to say nothing of what he'll probably inherit when his grandmother dies—provided that he marries with the old woman's approval. And her own nurse, if the nurse humors her sufficiently, might very well meet with that approval."

Helen's chin went up and a spot of indignant color leaped into either cheek.

"I resent that, Dr. Richard's!" she exclaimed. "You've no right—"

The doctor laughed disagreeably.

"Permit me to remind you," he said, "that you are here to assist me, not to hinder me by the furtherance of any little schemes of your own. Need I point out to you that if you do otherwise than what I wish, the consequences to yourself may be decidedly unpleasant?"

"Are you threatening me?"

"Threatening you?" His eyebrows rose. "My dear young woman, what a preposterous idea! I am merely warning you that unless you stick more closely to—er—business, I may find it necessary to remove you from the case, and to appoint another nurse to look after Mrs. Marsden. She herself would never tolerate incompetency if she came to learn about it—or fortune hunting."

Helen bit her full red underlip, but said nothing.

The doctor picked up his medical case again and turned toward the house.

"Come," he said over his shoulder. "We'll go see whether the old lady is awake yet."

"Just a minute, Doctor."

He half turned.

"Well?"

Helen didn't like to put the question to him, but she felt that she had to know; and there wasn't anybody else she could ask.

"If—if Mrs. Marsden should be declared mentally incapable," she began, finding difficulty in choosing just the right words, "would any will that she might make during her derangement be considered legal?"

"I haven't the faintest idea," he replied indifferently, "but I should imagine not. Why do you ask?"

"Because," Helen answered, "a lawyer came to see her today. I think she's getting him to draw up a will."

"A strange lawyer?" He was faintly amused. "That looks as though Ronnie, and not Ralph, is to be the heir to her portion of the estate. The pot of gold at the end of your particular rainbow seems to be diminishing, Miss Godwin."

The deliberate taunt in his voice stung her to what she would otherwise have left unsaid.

"It may interest you to know," she told him deliberately, "that the lawyer who came here was Stephen Carter."

"*What!*" This time he swung all the way around. "Great God! Carter's no ordinary lawyer; he's practically a—detective!"

"I know that."

Nurse and doctor eyed each other steadily for fully half a minute; then he observed:

"So that was what you meant when you said the old lady hadn't done any more talking *that you knew of.*"

"Perhaps." Helen permitted herself the faintest of smiles.

The doctor's expression was a mixture of fear and helpless rage. Then both vanished, and he flung back his head and began to laugh.

"Capital!" he exclaimed. "This may be the very best thing that could have happened. Let her tell Carter everything. With nothing to back up a story like that, she'll only convince him that she's crazy as a coot, and pave the way for—"

He broke off in mid-sentence.

"Come, Miss Godwin," he said with an abrupt resumption of his professional manner. "We'll go upstairs and have a look at our patient."

II.

Ronnie Marsden surveyed her reflection in the full-length mirror, and approved. She had exchanged the white linen tennis costume that she had been wearing in the afternoon for a dinner dress, also white. Ronnie generally wore white. It complemented the golden sun-bronze of her skin; and with all her boyishness, she was still feminine enough to take that into consideration.

Whistling a snatch of a Strauss waltz under her breath, she went out into the hall; then she stopped before her grandmother's door.

"Are you asleep, Gram?" she called softly.

"No, dear; come in."

Ronnie opened the door, and stepped into the room. Mrs. Marsden was lying on her bed, propped up with pillows. The light of the westering sun, slanting across her face, made it look like a delicate carving from old ivory.

Ronnie crossed to the window to draw the shade a trifle, but her grandmother stopped her.

"Leave it up, dear," she said. "I like to have the sunlight on my face. It makes me feel—more alive."

Ronnie dropped her hand from the shade. She came over and sat down on the chair beside her grandmother's bed.

"Was the doctor here today?" she inquired.

"Yes, he was here late this afternoon."

"What did he say?"

"Oh, the usual thing." The old lady smiled humorlessly. "That I'm to get plenty of rest, and avoid all excitement."

The suggestion of a shadow flitted across Ronnie's face.

"Any more nightmares, Gram?" she asked hesitantly.

Her grandmother shot her a quick, keen glance.

"You think I imagined those things; don't you, Ronnie?" she asked. "You don't believe me any more than the others do."

"Oh, no Gram," Ronnie defended herself, but a telltale flush suffused her cheeks. "It isn't that. It's only that—well, that sometimes a dream can be so vivid it seems as though it must have been a reality."

"Don't hedge," Mrs. Marsden commanded with a flash of spirit "I know what you all think." Then she added more quietly. "But I can't say that I blame you, or Ralph and the doctor, either. It must sound crazy to anyone who hears about it. Helen is the only one who believes me; and sometimes I suspect that she only pretends to in order to humor me."

Ronnie said nothing, but she couldn't control a slight contraction of her nostrils at mention of the nurse's name.

Her grandmother saw it, and asked:

"You don't like Helen, do you, Ronnie?"

"No, Gram; to be quite honest with you, I don't."

"Why?"

"Oh, I don't know." Ronnie groped around in her mind for some word with which to express the instinctive aversion that the nurse always aroused in her. "She's too—voracious. She has a way of looking at you—at anyone, I mean—as though she were going to eat you up."

"Your cousin, Ralph, wants to marry her."

"I suspected it would come to that."

"And you don't approve?" Mrs. Marsden was eyeing her grand-daughter intently, studying her every change of expression.

"It's hardly my place to approve or disapprove," Ronnie said steadily, but without returning the older woman's look. "Who Ralph marries is his own affair—and yours."

"But you think that Helen is deliberately trying to rope him in on account of the money," Mrs. Marsden observed. "Well, perhaps you're partly right, at that. I know the girl isn't just our sort." The snobbery in both words and tone was wholly unconscious. "But she won't be any worse for Ralph than he is for himself. Besides, I won't be here to look after him always, and it isn't fair to pass the responsibility along to you, Ronnie."

"Don't talk that way, Gram. It makes me feel all sort of cold inside."

"But it *isn't* fair," the old lady persisted. "You have your own life to live."

Ronnie said nothing.

"I see you're wearing a party dress this evening," her grandmother observed with one of her abrupt changes of subject. "Is it a special occasion?"

Ronnie smoothed a soft fold of her skirt.

"I'm going out to dinner with Whitney Hamilton," she replied a little self-consciously.

Mrs. Marsden studied her thoughtfully from beneath half closed lids; then:

"Ronnie," she inquired, "if Whitney were to ask you to marry him, what would be your answer?"

The girl looked away.

"He won't ask me to marry him," she said matter-of-factly.

"What makes you think so?"

"You know why, Gram."

"It may be different, after tonight," Mrs. Marsden said unexpectedly.

Ronnie looked around quickly.

"What do you mean?" she asked.

Her grandmother smiled.

"Wait and see," she said cryptically.

III.

Ralph Marsden came slowly down the stairs into the library. He was a somewhat pudgy young man, with a childish droop to the corners of his mouth. A lock of his heavy, taffy-colored hair had fallen across his forehead, and he paused to brush it back impatiently. Then he cast a searching glance around the room, only to discover that it was empty.

"Helen!" he called. There was a hint of querulousness in his voice. "Where are you, Helen?"

The screen door to the side porch opened, and Helen Godwin came into the room.

"Here I am, Ralph," she said. "I was outside getting a breath of air. Today has been stifling."

"You're telling me." He passed his hand for the second time across his glistening forehead, while his eyes swept in frank approval over the firm, rounded lines of the girl's figure, emphasized by the low-cut dress of clinging red near-silk that she now wore in place of her uniform. Helen saw the look, and it gratified her, even while at the same time something deep within her rebelled.

Ralph crossed the room, slipped an arm familiarly around her waist, and drew her out again upon the porch.

"Helen," he began with the abruptness which was his one inherited characteristic from his grandmother, "I've been thinking: It's not that Gram doesn't approve of you; it's simply that she can't make up her mind. So why don't you and I drive down to Virginia some night—say even tonight—and get married without saying anything to anybody? Gram would come around all right when we told her; I know she would."

"What about your cousin Ronnie?"

"The devil with Ronnie! She's not my guardian; Gram is."

Helen hesitated; then she withdrew herself from his encircling arm, and turned to face him.

"Ralph," she said, "we may as well look at this thing squarely. You know about those hallucinations your grandmother's been having for the past few months. Dr. Richards thinks that they may possibly be a forerunner of—something more serious. But whether they are or not, if you and I were to be married the way you suggest, Ronnie would seize upon them as an excuse to have your grandmother declared mentally incompetent of handling her affairs before she had a chance to turn your share of your grandfather's estate over to you. And you know what that would mean."

"Oh, Ronnie's not such a bad sort as all that," he protested. "She wouldn't—"

"That's what you think," Helen interrupted him. "I tell you, Ralph,

Ronnie's hated me ever since I came here. She knows how things stand between us, and she thinks I'm not good enough to become a Marsden." There was resentment in her voice; the instinctive resentment of the Have-Not's for the Have's. "And let me tell you another thing: She's been working upon your grandmother to disinherit you."

"Now, Helen, that's only a crazy idea you've got."

"Oh, is it?" the girl retorted. "Then listen to this: Today she had a lawyer here drawing up a will for her. Doesn't the fact that she called in an outsider, instead of having Ronnie do it, prove that Ronnie's to be the chief beneficiary?"

He remained silent for several seconds.

"If I thought that was true—" he muttered finally.

"Well, it *is* true," Helen pressed her advantage. "You can take my word for it. The only thing for us to do is to get your grandmother's full consent, and to have her turn over your share in the estate to you *before* we're married."

"Gram would never do that. She'd think it was just another stunt of mine to get hold of the money."

"Then," Helen said firmly, "we had both better forget about the whole thing."

"So you don't want me without the money." The querulousness was back in his voice again.

"Poor little rich boy!" Helen gave a light laugh, but it was fortunate that the deepening dusk on the porch partially hid her expression. "Of course I do! But I won't permit you to throw away your inheritance for me, and regret it later. You'd never be happy poor Ralph; you know that as well as I do."

He was silent for the space of a full minute; then he said:

"Suppose I could get Ronnie over on our side?"

"Get Ronnie—" Helen laughed again, this time in derision. "You'd have about as much chance of doing that," she commented, "as of flying to the moon."

"I'm not so sure about that."

Something in his tone made her strain her eyes to see him through the heavy shadows that surrounded them.

"What do you mean?" she asked.

"Ronnie would like to marry Whitney Hamilton. Well, it may rest with me whether she does or not."

She stared at him incredulously.

"You mean you can prove that he *did*—"

"Never mind," he cut in with heavy jocularity. "It doesn't always do for little girls to ask too many questions. Just leave everything to me, baby, and I'll guarantee that not only will Cousin Ronnie stop opposing us, but before I get through with her she'll actually be helping us, and be glad for the chance."

3

RATIOCINATION

(Tuesday, 7:30 p.m. to 8:30 p.m.)

1.

Stephen Carter mounted the three stone steps to the Heisy's front door and jerked the old-fashioned bell-pull. It gave with a startling unexpectedness that made him believe it had come loose in his hand; then, as he released it, it flew promptly back into position again as though possessed of a will of its own, while somewhere in the interior of the house echoed a sound melodiously reminiscent of a cowbell.

There followed a brief pause; then from the other side of the door came a faint rustle of sound, as though someone were endeavoring to peer through the lace curtain that covered the glass panel. After a few seconds more, a light sprang on, and the door was opened by a little old lady with two white curls dangling coquettishly over each ear.

Stephen removed his hat.

"Good evening, ma'am," he said. "I'd like to speak with the Misses Heisy, please."

The little old lady smiled up at him.

"I am Miss Phoebe Heisy," she told him. "Won't you come in, Mr. Carter?"

"You know my name?" he asked in surprise as he followed her through the hall and into the living room.

"Oh, yes," she answered brightly. "My sister Maime recognized you this afternoon when you were over at—" She broke off in confusion. "Just make yourself comfortable while I call Maime," she finished hurrriedly.

Stephen sat down upon a chair, which turned out to be unexpectedly slippery under its linen slip cover, and he had to brace his feet against the floor to keep from sliding off. He was inexperienced in the ways of Victorian horsehair furniture.

While he waited for Miss Phoebe to return he looked around him. The room was lighted by an old-fashioned glass lamp—originally oil, but now electrified in a concession to modernity—that bore a startling resemblance to an over-sized Silex coffee maker. Facing the open double doors into the hall and giving the effect of parting the

16

room in the middle like a part in a head of hair, an elaborate, white-tiled and pillared mantel, in the style of an earlier generation, embraced the ornamental iron grille of a hot air register. It was topped by a gilt-framed mirror as long as itself, which in turn was flanked by two crayon enlargements also in gilt frames, "our mom and our pap," Stephen concluded correctly, remembering a remark of Mrs. Marsden's that afternoon. "Our mom" had a mouth that looked slightly scalloped, like the crimped edges of a pie. "Our pap" had square whiskers and a somewhat startled expression, the latter probably being the fault of the photographer.

Before Stephen could observe more, the door at the rear of the room opened, and Miss Maime Heisy came in. Unlike her sister, she was tall and thin; and again unlike Miss Phoebe, she wore no co-quettish curls. Instead, her hair had been screwed up into a tight knot on the exact top of her head, reminding Stephen of the little knob on the lid of a silver coffee pot belonging to his grandmother.

"Good evening, Mr. Carter," she said primly; then to her sister, who had followed her into the room like a complaisant shadow: "Phoebe, take Mr. Carter's hat."

When the hat had been placed in the exact center of one of the room's half dozen or so small tables, both the Heisy girls sat down together upon a linen-covered sofa and clasped their hands in their laps. They moved in such perfect unison, it was as though they were operated by a single piece of clockwork.

Stephen also sat down again—this time without skidding.

"I don't guess it's going to be easy to explain just why I'm here," he began awkwardly. "Your neighbor, Mrs. Marsden, sent for me this afternoon—"

"Yes, we know," Miss Maime interrupted shamelessly. "We wondered whether she was planning to make a will."

Stephen felt as though a chair had been pulled from under him mentally. But at least she had given him a lead.

"To tell you the truth, that's just what she did want," he said as soon as he had recovered himself. "But it's a—a sort of peculiar will."

"How's it peculiar?" Miss Maime inquired with interest.

"This way: Instead of leaving her estate to members of her own family, she wants to leave it to a man who's no relation—"

"A *man!*" Miss Maime repeated, scandalized. "And at her age! Well, like our pap used to say, there's no fool like an old fool."

"Oh, it's nothing like that," Stephen hastened to explain. "This man is a friend of her grand-daughter's."

"Is it anyone we know?" Miss Phoebe ventured timidly.

"That I couldn't say, ma'am. But when a will is drawn up disinheriting the natural heirs, there's always the chance that one of them may try to break it on the grounds of undue influence or mental incompetency. And so I thought I'd better talk to some disinterested persons who know Mrs. Marsden intimately, just to make sure—"

"That she's in her right mind?" Miss Maime interrupted. "Well, you can take it from us, Mr. Carter, she is. Oh, I know there's been some talk lately about her being a little queer; but Mary Marsden is as sane as you or I. And if she's cutting that lazy, good-for-nothing grandson of hers out of her will, that proves it." There followed a fifteen minute dissertation upon Ralph Marsden and his "goings on," interspersed with philosophical utterances attributed to "our mom and our pap." At the end of it Stephen felt slightly dizzy.

"Then if you think Mrs. Marsden knows what she's about and won't regret her action later," he said as soon as he could inject a word of his own into the vocal torrent, "I'll go on with the drawing of the will. I feel sure I can trust the judgment of you ladies."

Miss Maime nodded importantly.

"You go right ahead," she said. Mrs. Marsden knows what she's doing, all right. But it does seem strange she should be cutting Ronnie out. Ronnie's a nice girl, not at all like her worthless cousin Ralph.

"Now if anybody should try to break the will," she rattled on without so much as pausing for breath, "it would be that Ralph. He's been trying to think up ways to get hold of the money his grandpap left in trust for him ever since old Mr. Marsden died three years ago. And there's another thing, Mr. Carter." She lowered her voice to a hoarse whisper. "There's something going on over there at the Marsdens' that's not just as it ought to be. I won't say that Ralph's mixed up in it, but then again I won't say that he's not. But if you're to be Mary Marsden's lawyer, you just keep your eyes open; that's all I've got to say."

She pressed her lips together after the last word in a way that made her look strikingly like the crayon enlargement of "our mom."

Stephen wondered what precisely she might mean by that, but before he could decide whether it would be diplomatic or even safe to ask, Miss Phoebe put a question.

"This young man who is to inherit"—she began with her usual timidity—"did you say he was a friend of Ronnie's, Mr. Carter?"

"Yes, ma'am," Stephen admitted, "I believe he is."

He hurriedly thanked the Heisy girls for their information and made his escape—it literally amounted to that—before Miss Maime could put the questions that he saw gleaming in her eye. After all, it was not a part of the scheme that he should tell who was to be the heir, but only who was not.

Miss Maime watched him from behind the lace curtains as he returned to his car.

"I wonder what ails that young man," she remarked. "He's leaning against the door of his automobile as though he'd been overcome by the heat; and it's not *that* hot out this evening."

Miss Phoebe didn't even hear; she was thinking about something else.

"Maime, do you know what?" she demanded excitedly. "I believe Mary Marsden's leavivng her money to Whitney!"

II.

Whitney Hamilton looked up from the moody contemplation of his dinner plate, suddenly conscious of the silence that had persisted for the past several minutes. His eyes met Ronnie's, which were regarding him with a half-smile.

"Sorry," he apologized. "I was just thinking."

"May I ask about what, Whitney?"

"Oh, nothing in particular." He attempted a brief laugh that failed to ring true. "I guess I'm just poor company tonight; you must try to forgive me."

But Ronnie wasn't to be deceived. Her intuition and understanding of the man had told her what his words had not, and the smile vanished from her eyes.

"Whitney, you've been remembering again," she accused him, but there was sorrow rather than rebuke in her voice. "And you promised me that you'd put all that behind you."

He shrugged helplessly.

"I know," he admitted, "and God knows I've tried! But it won't be put behind. Oh, I know that in the eyes of the law I've been proven innocent—thanks to you, Ronnie. But in the eyes of the public . . . ."

"Does it matter so much what the public thinks?"

"On my own account, no; but for you . . . ."

"For me, Whitney?"

He didn't realize himself what he was going to say next until the words had rushed out.

"You must have guessed, Ronnie!" he exclaimed, unable to keep his emotions under control any longer. "A dozen times during the past few months I've planned to ask you to marry me; I planned it again this evening. But always before I can speak, that shadow comes between us. How can I ask a woman to share my life, when I'll always be suspected of—"

She stopped him with a gesture.

"Don't," she said. Her voice was slightly unsteady. "I *did* guess, Whitney; and I guessed, too, why you were keeping silent. So long as you did, there was nothing much I could do about it; but now that you've spoken, you give me the right to speak, too."

She paused for a moment to get better control of herself; then she continued:

"Ever since Ralph got me to take your case six months ago, I've believed in your innocence. You know that, so I won't bother to tell you that what other people may think—if they do think it—means nothing to me. But if you honestly feel that we can't marry so long as this—this shadow hangs over you, then I won't try to persuade you otherwise; we wouldn't be happy if I did. However, there's something else we can do: We can find out the real truth, and thereby banish the shadow once and for all."

But he shook his head.

"I'm afraid it's no use," he said. "If the police, with all the facilities at their command, couldn't do it at the time, what chance have we got, now that nearly a year has elapsed since—I don't want to sound like a pessimist and a quitter, but we've got to face the facts. I had no right to say what I did just now. Instead of coming here after the trial was over, I should have gone away and let you forget me. It— it's what I've got to do now, Ronnie."

"No!" Ronnie leaned toward him across the table. . She looked remarkably like a younger edition of her grandmother when she set her chin in that determined fashion. "I suppose I'm being what Gram would call a brazen hussy, but I'm not going to let you. I've got a right to fight for my happiness—for both our happiness."

He smiled faintly.

"I wonder," he observed, "what your grandmother would think if she knew you were willing to marry—a jailbird."

"Gram does know. I mean"—she colored slightly—"she knows all about you; Ralph told her. But she believes in you, the same as I do.

"What if the police did fail in their efforts to solve the case?" Her voice became more earnest. "Somewhere there must be somebody who knows the real facts; and I'm going to find that person, and make him or her tell." She clenched her slim brown hand into a fist and brought it down upon the edge of the table, heedless of the surprised stare of a passing waiter. "I'm going to start at the beginning and go over everything again: the newspaper accounts, the court record of your trial, everything—until I find some little fact that will tell me who that person is. If you won't help me look for it, Whitney, then I'll do it alone; and I won't give up until I've found it—ever!"

"God knows I want to!" the man exclaimed with feeling. "If I thought there was a chance . . ."

Then his smile deepened, extending this time to his eyes. He reached across the table until his hand covered the girl's slim brown fist.

"Madame Counsellor," he said, "you've won your case. We're going to take that chance. We're fighting this thing through to a finish— together."

III.

Jefferson Carter glanced up from his desk as his younger brother came into the study.

"Hello, Steve," he said. "Haven't seen you since morning, Been busy?"

Stephen tossed his tropical straw hat to the top of the highboy that did duty as a filing cabinet, then sat down sideways in Jefferson's big armchair, with his legs dangling over one of the arms.

"Man, have I been having me a day!" he exclaimed. "Life's been just one old lady after another!"

"I always knew you were a lady-killer," Jefferson remarked, "but my impression was that your taste ran towards redheads under twenty-five. What goes on?"

"You know old Mrs. Marsden? Mrs. Leland Marsden?"

Jefferson nodded.

"Snappy old girl," he commented. "I used to look after her husband's legal affairs when he was alive; and hers, too, until I accepted public office two years ago. I don't know who she's got now for her lawyer."

"She's got me."

"Eh?" Jefferson Carter swung around in his swivel chair until he was facing his brother. "Steve, what are you leading up to?"

"I was just wondering," Stephen answered, studying the toe of one of his white oxfords where it dangled over the arm of the chair, "whether anyone would profit if it was proven that the old lady wasn't quite right in her mind."

"Whether—*what?*" Jefferson was staring incredulously. "Who gave you that idea?"

"She did."

"I see." Jefferson looked thoughtful; then he said:

"Yes, it might be conceivable that somebody would profit if Mrs. Marsden were found incapable of looking after her financial affairs. I'll tell you the conditions of Leland Marsden's will, and you can judge for yourself.

"The estate was divided into three parts. The first, including the house and about fifty thousand dollars in cash and securities, was left outright to Mrs. Marsden. The second, another fifty thousand in stocks—or it amounted to that much at the time the will was drawn up—went into a trust fund to be used by Marsden's physician—a man named Richards, I believe—for bacteriological research. The third portion, somewhere in the neighborhood of sixty thousand dollars, was divided equally between Marsden's grandson and granddaughter, but with this difference: While the girl received her share outright, the boy's went into a trust fund until the time of his marriage, when he's to receive the whole of it the same as his cousin did hers, provided he marries with his grandmother's consent and approval."

"And his grandma was put in charge of the trust fund?" Stephen asked.

"Not only that, but in charge of the trust fund for the doctor as well," Jefferson replied.

"What happens if old Mrs. Marsden should die, or become in some other way incapable of administering her trusteeship?"

Jefferson linked his fingers behind his head, leaned back in his chair and closed his eyes in an effort to visualize the document he had drawn up five years before.

"Let's see now," he said slowly. "In that case, the trust fund set aside for the doctor ceases to exist, and he comes into full control of the principal with no strings attached, while the granddaughter takes over the trusteeship of her cousin's inheritance."

"And what becomes of Ralph Marsden's share of the estate if he marries without his grandma's consent?"

"He gets ten thousand dollars cash, and the rest reverts to his cousin Veronica."

Stephen brought his feet down from the arm of the chair.

"Well, shut my mouth!" he exclaimed. "Why, that gives all three of them a right good motive for getting the old lady out of the way!"

Jefferson opened his eyes again.

"Now hold on a minute, Steve," he protested "You asked me whether anyone would profit if it was found that Mrs. Marsden was mentally incompetent, and I've told you. But that doesn't imply that any of these people would deliberately set out to prove her that way. Why, Dr. Richards is a reputable physician; and the girl, Veronica, is devoted to her grandmother. As for Ralph Marsden, I'll admit he's something of a bad lot—that was the reason for the trust fund in his case in the first place—but I don't believe he's an out-and-out rascal. Besides, he wouldn't be any better off with Ronnie managing his affairs than he is now with his grandmother."

"I guess you know he could have that clause of the will set aside, since Miss Ronnie stands to benefit by keeping him out of his money?"

Jefferson nodded.

"Yes," he admitted, "but I doubt he knows it."

"Any lawyer could tell him. Maybe even Miss Ronnie herself."

"I doubt if it would ever occur to Ronnie. She's primarily a criminal lawyer; and a damned good one, too, for a mere girl. Remember that case of the chap in Pittsburgh who was accused of poisoning his wife about six months ago?"

"I don't guess I do, offhand."

"You must have seen something about it in the papers; they played it up big enough at the time. Chap named Albert Hamilton was charged with having put poison in his wife's coffee. Seems they had a joint insurance policy in each other's favor. Well, Ronnie Marsden managed to get Hamilton off by raising the well known 'reasonable doubt.' How she did it the Lord alone knows. There were several women on the jury, and Hamilton was a personable sort of chap, so maybe that explains it.

"But that's neither here nor there," Jefferson interrupted himself to return to the original subject under discussion. "I don't know what old Mrs. Marsden's been telling you, Steve, to make you think that somebody's out to railroad her to the asylum; but if I were you, I wouldn't take it too seriously. Remember, she must be over seventy; and old people often get ideas of persecution, especially if they're semi-invalids, as she is. Why—"

He stopped, becoming aware that his brother was no longer listening to him.

"What's the matter?" he asked. It always made him suspicious when Stephen suddenly fell silent that way. Experience had taught him that these silences were generally the forerunners of some action that he would in all probability not approve of.

Stephen replied with a question of his own.

"Jeff, did this Albert Hamilton have a middle name?"

"A middle name?" Jefferson repeated in astonishment. "Good Lord! how should I know? Come to think of it, though, I believe the newspapers did mention one a couple of times, although I can't remember what it was. But what's that got to do with old Mrs. Marsden?"

"Nothing—I hope," Stephen answered. He knew now why the man he had seen that afternoon playing tennis with Ronnie Marsden had looked so familiar to him.

4

COUNTERPLOT

(Tuesday, 11:30 p.m. to 12 m.)

I.

Whitney Hamilton saw the light under the door of the upstairs sitting room, stopped and turned the knob.

"Phoebe," he accused the old lady, "you've been waiting up for me again. You'll lose your beauty sleep."

Miss Phoebe giggled a little.

"As if beauty sleep mattered at my age!" she deprecated. "I wanted to know, Whitney. Tonight was to be the night, wasn't it? Are—are you and Ronnie—"

He started to grin; then his face sobered.

"I'm hanged if I know exactly," he murmured, more as though he were trying to decide the point for himself than answering her question.

"You don't know whether you and Ronnie are engaged?"

He crossed the room and dropped, Indian fashion, upon the floor at her feet.

"I need someone to talk to tonight, Phoebe," he began; "someone who'll understand, and help me to see things straight. I never knew my own mother; she died when I was less than a year old. So would you—that is—"

If he had offered her the position of first lady of the land, she could not have been more thrilled or more flattered. She laid aside the coat that she had been mending—one of his, incidentally—and rested her hand upon his hair where is sprang back, with a little defiant lift, from his forehead.

"What is it, dear?" she asked.

Whitney was silent for several seconds; then he began awkwardly:

"Suppose that a—a chap wants to marry a girl, but knows he has no right to ask her because of—of certain conditions. The girl knows about these conditions, but insists that they make no difference to her, and that together they might even be able to overcome them. Has this chap got the right to—to—"

Miss Phoebe smiled gently.

"To trust the girl's judgment in the matter?" she finished for him.

24

"Yes, Whitney, I think he has. After all, money isn't everything. And besides, he may not always be poor."

"Oh, it isn't that," Whitney said quickly. "I'm not exactly—that is, this chap could support a wife all right. But—well, let's take a hypothetical case," he interrupted himself. "Suppose, for example, that this man had been accused of a crime. Even though he had been acquitted, he knows that the stigma of it will follow him as long as the identity of the real criminal remains unknown. Naturally, he can't ask the girl to share a life with him that will be forever under a cloud, even though he knows she's willing."

He paused, as though finding difficulty in expressing himself properly. Miss Phoebe said nothing, but waited patiently for him to continue.

"The girl believes that there may still be a chance of clearing up the mystery," he went on after a moment, "but the man knows that at best it can be only one chance in ten thousand. Has he the right to stake everything on such great odds—the girl's happiness as well as his own—or would it be better and more honorable for him to go away, and let her forget him?"

Miss Phoebe smiled a little secret smile of understanding. How naive he was, to think that she could not see through his little subterfuge of a "hypothetical case."

"Girls like Ronne don't forget, dear," she told him. "You owe it to her and to yourself to take that chance—to let her take it with you—even if it should be one in ten million. Some day, somewhere, the truth about your first wife's death will come out; it's bound to. You must remember that, Whitney."

He looked up in startled amazement.

"Phoebe!" he exclaimed. "You know?"

"Yes," she admitted. "I've known from the first. You see, Maime recognized you from your pictures in the papers."

II.

Ronnie Mareden ran lightly up the stairs to her room. It was funny how, since that talk with Whitney, everything seemed so changed. Before it had been as though she were living in a sort of temporary world, with nothing certain from one day to the next. Now she could see ahead; could make plans. It was true that those plans would have to include a long, hard fight, but she didn't care; in fact, she actually gloried in the prospect. Together she and Whitney would win through in the end; they had to.

In the morning she'd start going over all the records of the case again: the testimony of the various witnesses at the trial, the newspaper accounts before that, everything that might possibly furnish her with a lead. Somewhere there must be something that would point the way to the truth—perhaps some little, seemingly unimportant detail that had been overlooked before—and if she searched hard enough and long enough, she would be bound to find it.

She ran over rapidly in her mind the principal facts of the case. Ten months before Whitney Hamilton's wife, Ruth, had died under circumstances so undeniably peculiar that the doctor who had been called to attend her had refused to sign the death certificate. An autopsy had been held, at which it was discovered that death had been caused by one of the barbital poisons, apparently administered in a cup of coffee. Police investigation had followed, and the joint insurance policy had come to light. As a result, Whitney had been arrested and charged with his wife's murder.

It had been Ralph Marsden who had gotten Ronnie, then just a year out of law school, to take the case for the defense. Odd, she thought now, that Ralph, who had never seemed to have a thought for anyone but himself in all his life, should have done this. He had been a frequent visitor to Pittsburgh in those days; and Ronnie had suspected that the attraction had been some feminine member of the ultra gay set with which the Hamiltons—or rather Ruth; Whitney had never cared particularly for any kind of social life—had traveled.

At first the case had seemed hopeless. The prosecution had been able able to show both motive and opportunity; opportunity in the fact, admitted by Whitney himself, that he and Ruth had been alone together on the fatal evening when she had drunk the poisoned coffee, and motive in the damning evidence of the insurance policy.

Whitney had been too grief-stricken over the death of his wife to be of much assistance in formulating his own defense, so Ronnie had turned to Ruth's former associates in the hope of finding a lead there. But she had met with disappointment. Ruth Hamilton, younger than her husband by almost ten years, had lived entirely for pleasure. Her butterfly nature had been too shallow to form either deep friend-ships or deep enmities. Consequently, Ronnie had been unable to discover anything in the girl's life that might have furnished an explanation of her death.

At last, after getting as many postponements of the trial as she dared, Ronnie had based her defense on two points: First, that the police had failed in their efforts to prove that Whitney had purchased the poison or had had other access to it; and second, that Ruth Hamilton herself had prepared the coffee in which the poison had been administered. It had been negative evidence at best, but it had been sufficient to create a reasonable doubt in the minds of the jury, who, after forty-eight hours of deliberation, had finally brought in a verdict of not guilty.

After the close of the trial Whitney's one thought had been to get away from the scene of his unhappiness and to forget, if possible, the torture of the past six months; and he had turned instinctively to the two people who had stood by him in his trouble: his lawyer and his erstwhile friend, Ralph Marsden. Ronnie, not entirely unselfishly, had suggested Ralph's and her home town as a place of retreat, since it was small enough to furnish the quiet he sought, yet not so small that a stranger would appear conspicuous. Whitney had seized upon the suggestion with almost pathetic eagerness; and in a naive attempt to conceal his identity without resorting to actual deception had dropped his first name, Albert, which the newspapers had used throughout the trial. Then, in the weeks of quiet summer that had followed—

A knock at her door broke in across Ronnie's thoughts.

"Who is it?" she called without rising from her chair.

"It's Ralph," her cousin's voice answered. "You haven't gone to bed yet, have you, Ron?"

"No," she replied without enthusiasm. "Come in."

He opened the door, but remained standing on the threshold.

"Maybe we'd better go downstairs to the library," he suggested. "There's something I want to talk to you about; and if we stay up here, we're liable to disturb Gram."

"All right." Ronnie rose and followed him from the room. She wondered, however, whether his desire to go downstairs to talk wasn't less solicitude for his grandmother than fear lest the old lady might overhear whatever it was he had to say.

When they reached the library Ralph crossed to one of the leather-upholstered chairs; but instead of sitting in it, he remained standing with his arms folded across its back. Ronnie, watching him, noticed that his face was flushed, and that he avoided meeting her eyes.

"Ralph," she accused him, "you've been drinking again."

He jerked a shoulder impatiently.

"Well, what if I have?" he demanded with a touch of defiance. "Anyway, it was only one or two to help me think. But it's not me we're here to discuss; it's you."

"I?"

"You *and* I, to be exact. Ronnie, you know I want to marry Helen, and—"

She stopped him with a gesture.

"Wait, Ralph," she said. "We've been all over this before. I told you that if Gram wanted to give her consent to your marriage, that was her business, but I won't try to influence her. That's final."

"Maybe it is, and then again maybe you'll change your tune when you hear what I've got to say. Did it ever occur to you, Ronnie, that you and I may be in pretty much the same boat?"

"I don't know what you mean."

"We both want to get married, but something stands in the way. Oh, don't get coy," as he saw that she was about to speak. "I know how matters are between you and Whit Hamilton. And I know, too, that he won't ask you to marry him so long as suspicion of Ruth's death hangs over him. Well, suppose I could fix things up for you. Would you help me in return?"

"Ralph, what are you getting at?" Ronnie demanded suspiciously, but she was unable to keep a note of sudden hope out of her voice. Her cousin noticed it, and grinned with satisfaction.

"I thought that would make you sit up and take notice," he observed. "Well, here's my proposition: You help me get Gram's consent to marry Helen, and make her turn my share of Gramp's money over to me at once. Then you promise to see to it that when she dies, I get the house here and half of what goes with it. I could ask for it all, but I'll be generous and let you keep half. In return, I promise to—"

"Ralph, are you out of your mind?" Ronnie interrupted. "Bargaining over Gram's money when—when she's still alive! I'm ashamed of you."

"Oh, stow it!" he exclaimed impatiently. "I can't see how it's any worse to talk about it now than it would be after she's dead. But of course, if you're not interested in clearing your precious Whitney's name—"

That caught her attention, just as he had known it would.

"What is it you know?" she demanded. "Ralph, tell me!"

"I know how Ruth Hamilton was killed; and what's more, I can produce written proof."

She searched his face, trying to make up her mind whether or not he was lying.

"I don't believe you," she said finally.

"Oh, no?" He thrust his hand into his trousers pocket and brought out a letter in a worn and soiled envelope. "Then take a look at this. No, I'll hold it," as Ronnie put out her hand to take the letter. "You can read it that way."

He withdrew the enclosure from its envelope, unfolded it and held it up. Ronnie, with her hands clasped behind her like a child playing a parlor game, stood in front of him and read:

Ralph dearest,
    By the time you get this, it will probably be all over. You remember the stuff you bought for me in Scranton to poison the dog? Well, I've decided to use it, but not on old Rover.
    Oh, I know how horrified you were when I mentioned this to you two weeks ago, and how you told me I mustn't think of such things, even as a joke. But I wasn't joking, and you weren't

*really horrified, were you, dearest? You only didn't want to
know anything about it in advance. Well, you won't; because,
as I said at the beginning of this letter, by the time you read this
it will be all over.*

*I've decided to put it in his coffee tomorrow at dinner, when
the maid has her afternoon off. It's really the only way, because
I know he would never consent to a divorce. And besides, what
would your grandmother say to your marrying a divorcee?*

*After it's all over and a few months have passed, we can be
married—perhaps even with your grandmother's consent. But
if we can't get that, there will still be the insurance money—
twenty-five thousand dollars for natural death; fifty thousand in
case of accident. And this will most certainly be an accident so
far as Whitney is concerned.*

*Perhaps I am being indiscreet in writing this letter, so you had
better destroy it as soon as you've read it. But think of it, Ralph
darling: soon we will be together always, with no one to stand
between us!*

All my love,

Ruth.

The last few words seemed to run together before Ronnie's eyes,
and she had to lean against the side of the chair to steady herself.

"Ralph!" she gasped in stark horror. "You—you— Oh, Ralph!"

He refolded the letter quickly and thrust it back into his pocket
without bothering first to return it to its envelope.

"Don't look at me like that, Ronnie!" he exclaimed, his shell of
self-satisfaction pierced by the expression he saw in her eyes. "I swear
to God I didn't know what she wanted with that poison when I got
it for her! I'd have stopped her if there'd been time. But then, when
she got the coffee cups mixed, which is what she must have done—"

But Ronnie wasn't even listening to his feeble protestations. Something else was foremost in her mind.

"Ralph!" she repeated, still in that tone of incredulous horror.
"You and Ruth Hamilton were—and Whitney was your friend!"

It was typical of the man that he should resent this more than he
had resented what he'd thought would be her charge of his complicity
in the contemplated crime.

"Whitney Hamilton was *not* my friend!" he flared. "I only met
him two or three times at Ruth's parties. And anyway, he never ap-
preciated her—him with his fishing and camping trips! Ruth wanted
fun—bright lights; and when he wouldn't show her any, he had to
put up with the consequences. Oh, don't be so damned righteous,
Ronnie!" he lashed out as he saw that her expression did not alter.
"Suppose cases had been reversed: Suppose you had met Whitney

before Ruth's death instead of afterwards. Would the fact that he was married have made any difference in your feeling for him?"

"No, I suppose it wouldn't," Ronnie admitted honestly. "But it would have made a great deal of difference in my actions. However, that isn't all, Ralph. You must have received this letter the same day Ruth Hamilton died; and so you knew the truth about her death from the very beginning. But you let Whitney be charged with her murder and be put on trial for his life, and you never said a word!"

"I'd have told you if he'd been convicted," he defended himself. "Use your head, Ronnie. Why else do you think I saved that letter?"

She was silent for the space of a few seconds; then she said slowly:

"I suppose I can believe that. Anyway, I want to. But a word from you could have saved him from all that sickening horror of the trial, and you didn't speak it. You let an innocent man go through all those months of shame and torture, because you were too cowardly to admit that you had been carrying on a sordid intrigue with his wife. I'll never forgive you for that, Ralph; never!"

He read into her last sentence a refusal to accede to his plan; and his sullen anger, which had been mounting before, suddenly gave place to apprehension.

"Ronnie, that's not fair!" he whined, taking a step toward her. "I'll admit I may have been a bit of a rotter where Ruth was concerned, but I'm not as bad as you're trying to make me appear. I— I had my reasons for not showing that letter."

"Very well, then; what were they?"

He cast frantically about in his mind for an explanation and, to his own surprise, found one.

"You know how hard Whitney took Ruth's death," he began. "He was crazy about her. You even used that as one of your points in your summation to the jury. Well, suppose he'd found out that she— that I— Oh, damn it all, you know what I'm trying to say. He couldn't have taken it, Ron. He might even have tried to kill himself. Now do you understand why I kept quiet?"

"Yes, I understand," Ronnie said faintly through lips that had suddenly grown cold and white. It was true, what Ralph had just said. Whitney had loved Ruth very much, in spite of the differences in their temperaments; still held an affection for her memory. Ronnie knew that, and would not have had it otherwise. But what, under the circumstances, would be his reaction if he were to learn now of Ruth's unfaithfulness? Would the proof of his innocence in her death compensate for the hurt of that knowledge? Whitney was an idealist. Perhaps the destruction of his faith in one woman might even—

Ralph, misinterpreting his cousin's silence, broke in upon it.

"You see my point now, don't you, Ronnie?" he asked. "And you'll help me?"

"What?" Ronnie came back to her surroundings with a start. "What did you say, Ralph?"

"I said, you'll help me with Gram, won't you?" he repeated impatiently. "You'll get her to consent to my marrying Helen, and you'll see to it that I get the house and my half of everything later, if I give you this letter?"

Ronnie knew that she should have been angry with him for his base effrontery, but she was too confused, too miserable, to feel any other emotion. Even the outrageousness of his conduct now and at the time of the trial seemed suddenly insignificant in view of the problem that confronted her.

"I—I don't know," she replied without looking at him. "I've got to have time—time to think."

Ralph tossed back his blond forelock with an angry hand.

"Of course," he said with what was intended to be heavy sarcasm, "if you think more of the money than you do of the man you want to marry. . . ."

This time she looked him full in the face; and although she was almost a head shorter than he, when she addressed him it was as though she spoke from a great height above him.

"Fool!" she said. "It's not myself I'm thinking of; it's Whitney. I've got to decide where his happiness lies."

Ralph watched her in muddled perplexity as she turned and slowly ascended the stairs again. Then abruptly he swore with all the impotent fury of a man whose carefully blown bubble of intrigue has unexpectedly burst in his face. He had just realized that, in his attempt to justify himself, he had overshot his own mark.

5

HALLUCINATION

(Wednesday, 10 a.m. to 10:45 a.m.)

I.

The front door of the Marsden house was opened for Stephen not by the trim little parlor maid who had answered his ring the preceding afternoon, but by the bold-eyed nurse.

"You're Mrs. Marsden's lawyer, aren't you?" she asked, flashing him a red-lipped smile that Stephen felt she must turn on and off like a traffic light. "I'll have to ask you to wait for a few minutes in the drawing room, Mr. Carter. Dr. Richards is with Mrs. Marsden just now."

She led the way into a large room whose drawn venetian blinds rendered it pleasantly cool in comparison to the heat of the sun outside.

"I'll call you as soon as the doctor leaves," she promised, and withdrew with another automatic flash of the smile.

Stephen, wondering absently whether that particular red was meant to imply go or stop, sat down in the nearest chair and placed his briefcase on the floor beside him. He would have liked to ask whether the doctor's visit was merely a routine affair, or whether it signified some special indisposition on the part of his client; but the nurse had withdrawn before he had been able to frame the question.

After about five minutes of waiting he heard footsteps descending the stairs, then the sound of a man's voice in the room across the hall.

"The main thing, Miss Godwin," it was saying in dryly professional tones, "is to keep her quiet. Pretend to believe her about these hallucinations if she starts talking about them again; and whatever you do, don't let her become excited. There's the heart condition to be considered, you know."

"I'll remember that, Doctor," the nurse's voice answered. "And by the way, her lawyer is waiting to see her now. Shall I allow him to go up?"

"H'm." The sound was the vocal counterpart of a worried frown. "He's here now, you say? Perhaps I'd better have a word with him first."

The footsteps came across the hall to the room where Stephen

32

was waiting. The nurse was the first to put in an appearance.

"This is Dr. Richards, Mr. Carter," she said, indicating the little man who followed immediately behind her. "He would like to speak with you before I take you up to Mrs. Marsden."

"Good morning, sir," the doctor said with a touch of professional pomposity. He extended a hand which proved to be unexpectedly soft and hot.

Stephen studied the chubby, childish face with its disconcerting Van Dyke, and decided promptly that he didn't like the man.

"Good morning, Doctor," he responded, hoping that his feelings didn't color his voice. "I hope Mrs. Marsden isn't feeling bad today?"

Dr. Richards permitted himself a slight, non-committal shrug.

"It's nothing serious," he replied. "She's merely been having—" He broke off abruptly, as though fearing that he had been upon the point of a professional indiscretion. "Forgive me if I appear impertinent, Mr. Carter,' he began again, "but is your business with Mrs. Marsden anything of—er—an important nature?"

"It's important to her, I guess," Stephen answered with equal professional caution.

The doctor's prominent eyes flickered for the barest instant; then he said:

"Perhaps, since you are her lawyer, I had better take you into my confidence the same as though you were a member of the family. Mrs. Marsden has been suffering lately from—let us say, a slight mental indisposition, which sometimes leads her to make some most amazing statements of what she believes to be fact. Quite often these statements are—ah—of a rather startling nature, and may convey a misleading impression to anyone unacquainted with her condition. I feel that, since you are to have charge of her legal affairs, you should be prepared for any—er—slight idiosyncracies."

"You mean," Stephen asked baldly, "that she's a little crazy?"

"Oh, no, no," the doctor denied at once. "Nothing like that. The word 'crazy' implies complete mental derangement, which most certainly does not exist in Mrs. Marsden's case and, I hope, never will." He frowned delicately, like a man who does not wish to say too much, yet fears that he may not have said enough. "Her trouble appears to be occasional attacks of visual hallucination," he finished.

"She's been seeing things?"

"You might call it that." The bearded lips parted in the barest suggestion of a smile.

"Dr. Richards," Stephen said, "you say that you feel I should know about this, since I'm to be in charge of Mrs. Marsden's legal affairs. Does that mean that you consider her mentally incompetent?"

For some reason the question appeared to disconcert the doctor. His gaze shifted to the tiger's-eye ring on his finger, as though attracted by the play of light inside the stone.

"Not at all!" he denied quickly—too quickly, Stephen thought. "Not being a specialist in mental diseases myself, I would not attempt to diagnose her condition beyond what I have already said. I merely thought that—er—as a matter of general principle, you should be prepared for any irregularities in her conduct or conversation."

"I see." Stephen smiled ingenuously. "I'll remember what you've told me, Doctor."

"And you won't permit her to become excited? Her heart, you know."

"I don't guess there's anything about signing a will that might excite her," Stephen observed.

"No, of course not," the doctor agreed. His expression seemed to say, "So that's all she wants you for!" and to say it with relief.

He murmured some polite banality and withdrew. Stephen picked up his briefcase automatically and followed the nurse across the hall and up the stairs.

·But three ideas had taken possession of his mind, and were refusing to be dislodged. The first was that the conversation between the doctor and the nurse before they came into the room where he was had been deliberately carried on for his benefit; the second, that Dr. Richards had wanted to impress upon his mind that Mrs. Marsden's statements were not to be relied upon; and the third, that the doctor had been afraid that his, Stephen's, presence in the house might augur something less innocuous than the mere signing of a will.

II.

Mrs. Marsden affixed her signature to the bottom of the will; then she lay back in her chair and watched Helen Godwin and the little parlor maid sign after her as witnesses. She remained so until they had left the room; then she addressed Stephen.

"You're sure, now, that that will can't be broken?" she demanded.

"Yes, ma'am," he answered emphatically. "Why, that will's so foolproof I couldn't even break it myself."

The old lady's eyes flickered with momentary amusement, but sobered almost at once.

"All right," she said. "Now suppose you tell me what Richards was whispering to you about me down there in the lower hall."

Stephen was momentarily disconcerted by this unexpected attack.

"He—he told me I wasn't to let you get excited," he stammered.

"That wasn't all he said. He told you that I was losing my mind. Didn't he?"

"Oh, no, ma'am." Stephen hesitated, stole a quick glance at the keen old face in front of him and decided to risk the whole truth. "He said that you'd been having what he called visual hallucinations," he finished.

Mrs. Marsden smiled thinly.

"So that's the way he puts it," she observed. "And what did you say?"

"I said I'd remember what he told me."

"Meaning . . . ?"

"That I'd form my own opinion."

"And that opinion is—"

"It isn't formed yet, ma'am," he answered honestly. "I haven't known you long enough."

The old lady chuckled.

"I see I've made no mistake in choosing you for my lawyer," she commented. "You'll be honest with me, and that's the main thing I want." She sat up abruptly in her chair, clasping both hands about the knob of her cane. "So I'm going to be equally honest with you," she announced. "I *have* been having hallucinations; or at least that's what the rest of them believe. But I'm convinced that somebody in this house is trying to make it appear that I'm losing my mind."

Stephen did not pretend surprise.

"Have you any idea which one may be doing that, Mrs. Marsden?" he inquired.

The old lady considered.

"I'd say it was that scalawag Ralph," she replied, "except that, even if he did get me put away, he wouldn't be any better off than he is now; for then Ronnie would become his legal guardian. You know the terms of my late husband's will?" she interrupted herself to ask.

"Yes, ma'am," Stephen answered. "Jeff told me last night."

Again she chuckled, this time with a touch of grimness.

"So you've been a jump ahead of me all the time," she observed. "Well, it saves me the trouble of making a long and involved explanation. But what do you think, Stephen? Which one of them has the most motive to have me declared incompetent to handle my own affairs?"

"Well," Stephen replied judiciously, "they've all got about equal motive: Ralph to get control of the money his grandpa left him— he could break that clause in the will naming Miss Ronnie as his guardian if anything happened to you, since he could show that it was to her interest to keep him out of his inheritance; Miss Ronnie, to get control of all of her grandpa's estate, and probably yours as well; and Dr. Richards, to get hold of the principal of that trust fund that your husband set aside for him for scientific research. It all depends upon which one feels the greatest urge to act on his motive."

Mrs. Marsden drew in her underlip thoughtfully.

"You can rule Ronnie out," she said. "She's the one person in the house that I can trust, even if she does believe that the things I see are only nightmares. And Ralph doesn't have brains enough to know about breaking the will, although he'd do it in a minute if he thought of it. As for Richards—"

"Yes?" Stephen prompted as she hesitated.

"I suppose he would like to get his fingers on that fifty thousand dollars," she admitted, "and I don't imagine it would be entirely for scientific research, either. There were some pretty fishy items in that last report he made to me, and I told him so. Still, he isn't here at night, and it's then that I see the figure."

"The figure?"

"That's the hallucination Richards was telling you about." Her lips creased themselves into a mirthless smile. "A figure all in white, like the conventional idea of a ghost, that comes and stands at the foot of my bed and just looks at me. Oh, I know it sounds utterly ridiculous; but that's the clever part of it. It makes me look such a perfect fool when I talk about it."

"Haven't you ever called for help when you saw it?"

"Of course I have," she retorted impatiently. "But it always manages to get away before anybody can reach me. Although last night," she added reminiscently, "I thought sure that Helen would see it, because instead of going out into the hall or into the bathroom as it generally does, it went into her room, which communicates with mine. But she was asleep, and didn't see anything."

Stephen looked decidedly interested.

"By 'Helen,' you mean your nurse?" he asked.

But before Mrs. Marsden could answer the door to the hall opened, and the nurse herself came into the room.

"I'm afraid you're tiring yourself, Mrs. Marsden," she began. There was professional solicitude in her voice, and nothing more; but her color, Stephen noted, was just a shade too high not to have been caused by some more personal emotion. "Remember, you didn't sleep well last night. If you have more business to discuss with Mr. Carter, perhaps he could come back again when you are feeling better."

The old lady looked as though she were about to protest this interruption, but apparently she changed her mind.

"Perhaps you're right, Helen," she said, accenting the girl's name just a shade, and thereby supplying the answer to Stephen's question. "I do feel a little tired. Fetch me a glass of water, and I'll take one of my headache tablets."

She waited until she had left the room again, then she beckoned Stephen to her.

"Do you think she's mixed up in it?" she asked swiftly.

He nodded.

"She's almost got to be, if the figure went into her room and she claimed she didn't see it," he replied. "Did Dr. Richards recommend her?"

"Yes," she answered. "But Ralph wants to marry her, so she might be working with either of them."

Stephen made no comment. Instead he asked:

"Mrs. Marsden, do you know how to operate a camera?"

"Heavens, yes!" she replied. "My husband used to be quite an amateur photographer, and he taught me a lot about the things."

"Then I'm going to come back this evening and bring you a camera fitted with special infra-red film for taking pictures in the dark," he went on, speaking rapidly before the nurse should return. "Keep it concealed in your bed; and the next time this white figure appears, don't let it know you see it, but try to make a picture of it if you can. Then telephone for me at once, and we'll see what we've got."

The old lady's eyes shone with excitement.

"Capital!" she exclaimed. "Once we've got a picture of the thing, it'll prove I'm not going out of my mind."

"It may prove a lot more than that," he said; then, as he detected an almost imperceptible foot-fall in the hall: "And I wouldn't worry too much about these things, ma'am. As Miss Ronnie says, they're most likely just bad dreams."

When Nurse Godwin came into the room a second or two later he was busily fastening the straps on his briefcase preparatory to taking his departure.

6

ACCUSATION

(Wednesday, 10:45 a.m. to 2:15 p.m.)

I.

Miss Phoebe beckoned Ronnie to her across the garden.

"My dear," she said, "allow me to be one of the first to wish you all happiness. Whitney told me last night after he came home, and —why, Ronnie, what's the matter?" she broke off in frank bewilderment. "You're crying!"

Ronnie had turned away her face.

"Miss Phoebe," she asked, fighting to keep her voice steady, "how much did Whitney tell you?"

"Everything," Miss Phoebe replied eagerly. "Although I knew most of it long ago—about his trouble, I mean. Maime recognized him the day he came, but we didn't say anything, because we believed in him the same as you did, and we knew he didn't want to talk about it. But you mustn't let yourself become discouraged, dear," she went on sympathetically. "Even if it does take a long time to find out the thing you both want to know, as our pap used to say, 'Truth crushed to earth shall rise again. . . .' "

Ronnie didn't bother to inform her that it had been William Cullen Bryant, and not "our pap," who had first said that.

"I've already found out the truth, Miss Phoebe," she said brokenly, "and I'm afraid it means that Whitney and I can never be happy. Not ever."

Miss Phoebe stared in puzzled incredulity; then she unfastened the wire gate in the hedge that separated the two gardens.

"Come over her, child, and tell me all about it," she invited. "You'll feel better for talking; and maybe I can think of something that will help."

Ronnie permitted herself to be led across the lawn to one of the straight-backed wicker rockers on the Heisy's side porch, where, after one or two false starts, she poured out her whole story. When she arrived at the final chapter embracing Ralph's involvement in the tragedy of Ruth Hamilton's death and the letter he had shown to Ronnie the night before, poor Miss Phoebe's expression became a mixture of scandalization and horror. In her nice, chaste old mind,

38

the breaking of the seventh commandment was a much more shameful thing than the breaking of the sixth.

"So you see, Miss Phoebe," Ronnie concluded, all unconscious of the tumult of outraged emotions she had aroused in the maidenly breast opposite her, "now that I do know the truth, it—it's almost worse than it was before. Whitney adored Ruth; believed in her. Have I the right to destroy all that by telling him that—that—"

Miss Phoebe understood, perhaps even better than Ronnie herself; and being more than twice Ronnie's age, she was able to view the situation in better perspective.

"What you really mean, my dear," she said, rocking slowly back and forth as she talked, "is that you're afraid the clearing of his name will not compensate for the hurt that the knowledge of the truth must bring with it. But look at it this way, Ronnie: Whitney can't live in the past; the fact that he now wants to marry you proves that he wouldn't choose to even if he could. I know the hurt and disillusionment will seem cruel at first, but sometimes we must be cruel in order to be kind. You must decide, Ronnie, which is the more important to him: his past memories or his future happiness. Is it such a hard decision to make?"

"But," Ronnie asked uncertainly, "could I be sure that knowing would bring him happiness? We almost always hate the people who destroy our ideals. Maybe if I told him, he—he might even come to hate me!"

But Miss Phoebe shook her head.

"No, dear," she said. "Whitney isn't like that. But I can understand your not wanting to be the one to tell him, under the circumstances. Let me think; perhaps we can find another way."

"You won't have to, Phoebe," Whitney's voice spoke unexpectedly from the doorway behind them. "I've already heard."

Miss Phoebe gave a little startled squeal; Ronnie was incapable of any sound.

"It's all right, Ronnie," he said. He crossed to her and seated himself upon the arm of her chair. "I appreciate your decency in not wanting to be the one to tell me, and I love you all the more for it. But I've suspected something of the truth for a long time; only I had no idea that Ralph was the man, nor that—that the coffee that night was intended for me. I thought it might have been part of a suicide pact. I should have known that Ruth would never have had the nerve for anything like that."

"Whitney, I—I'm sorry," Ronnie stammered. It seemed like an inadequate thing to say, but she could think of nothing better.

He smiled down at her.

"Don't be," he said. "I wanted to know the truth; that's why, when I heard my name mentioned out here and realized what you

and Phoebe were talking about, I decided I'd better stay and listen."
He glanced briefly at the old lady, who was drinking in the scene
with undisguised avidity.

"Oh, I'll admit it hurts," he went on honestly. "It always hurts,
I suppose, to find out that one's been worshipping for years at the
feet of a false idol. But it isn't nearly so painful as you thought
it would be—or as I thought, either, for that matter. But there's
one more thing I've got to know, Ronnie: You told Phoebe that
Ralph said he'd strike a bargain with you for that letter. What was
to have been your part of that bargain?"

"He wanted me to get Gram's consent to his marrying Helen Godwin," Ronnie replied. She felt vaguely embarrassed at having to admit
Ralph's cupidity. "And—and to see to it that he gets the house and
one half of Gram's estate when she dies."

"Oh, no!" Miss Phoebe protested, joining in the conversation for
the first time. "You mustn't do that, Ronnie! You can't!"

"You're jolly well right she can't, Phoebe!" Whitney exclaimed
grimly. "I'll not be bought and paid for by anybody, not even by
Ronnie. Particularly when Ralph's doing the selling." He rose
purposefully.

Ronnie caught hold of his arm, staying him.

"Whitney, where are you going?" she demanded, alarmed by his
expression and the tone of his voice.

He patted her hand reassuringly, then removed it gently from
his arm.

"After Ralph," he answered. "And that letter."

II.

Jefferson Carter rose to shake hands with the visitor whom his secretary had just shown into his private office.

"Glad to see you, Ralph," he said, although that was something of
an overstatement. "I haven't laid eyes on you since—let's see—it
must have been since shortly after your grandfather's funeral."

Ralph Marsden nodded without enthusiasm. The subject of his
late grandfather was, unfortunately, not a popular one with him.

"Hello, Jeff," he said. He spoke with some difficulty, due to a
badly swollen lip and a missing tooth. "Got a minute to spare? I'd
like to ask your advice on what I can do in a certain matter."

Jefferson waved him to a chair, but his eyes narrowed ever so
slightly as he pushed a box of cigarettes across the desk in Ralph's
direction.

"I'll be glad to give you any advice I can," he replied. "But if it's
your grandfather's will again, I can only repeat what I told you before: That will is wholly valid and foolproof; and any attempt you

might make to have it overthrown in a court fight would only result in a decision against you. I'm sorry for your sake, but that's how it is."

Ralph raised his hand in a gesture of denial.

"It's not the will," he said. "This is another matter entirely; something that, I believe, ought to come under your province as district attorney."

Jefferson paused in the act of lighting a cigarette to shoot him a swift, inquiring glance, which took in the swollen lip, several minor cuts and bruises, and finally came to rest upon a black eye that even Helen Godwin's expert ministrations had been unable to do much about.

"All right," he said laconically. "Let's have it."

Ralph lowered his own gaze to his carefully manicured fingernails, whose shining elegance was marred somewhat by the skinned knuckles above them. ·

"You remember the Hamilton case in Pittsburgh a couple of months ago?" he began abruptly. "Fellow accused of poisoning his wife. I happened to know them both; and since Hamilton was in too much of a blue funk to look after his own interests, I got my cousin Veronica to take his case. She got him off."

"Yes, I know," Jefferson nodded. He was remembering Stephen's question about Albert Whitney Hamilton the evening before, and wondering whether there wouldn't prove to be a tie-up between it and Ralph's visit. "Your cousin did a brilliant piece of work on that case."

Ralph smiled sourly.

"Yes," he agreed. "The only trouble is she wouldn't realize when her job was finished."

"What's that supposed to imply?"

"Well, Ronnie always has been a champion of whoever she considers the underdog. So when the case was over and Hamilton wanted to get away somewhere to try to forget it all, she suggested that he come here, where nobody would know him. Luckily for him, the newspapers had always referred to him by his first name, Albert, which he never used; so when he came here calling himself Whitney Hamilton, it didn't mean anything to anybody."

"What's all this got to do with your visit here this morning?" Jefferson inquired with a touch of impatience.

Ralph decided that he had better get to the point.

"It's this," he replied. "Recently Hamilton's gotten it into his head—or pretends to have—that I was playing around with his wife."

"And were you?"

Ralph's already florid countenance flushed to an even darker red, and he made as if to rise from his chair.

"Look here, Carter," he blustered, "I didn't come down here to be insulted. I—"

"Oh, sit down," Jefferson snapped, "and say whatever it is you've got to say. You've already been talking five minutes without telling me anything." But he was thinking privately how Stephen had once remarked that a man gets angrier when an accusation is the truth than when it isn't.

Ralph dropped back into his chair again.

"Sorry I let go that way," he muttered. "The truth is, I'm still pretty much upset—nervously and emotionally, you know. I had a— a rather unpleasant encounter with Hamilton this morning." .

"During which he hung on you that beautiful shiner you're wearing?"

"He struck me without warning," Ralph said with dignity. "But that's why I'm here, Jeff, I want to know what can be done about it."

Jefferson suppressed a smile.

"Raw beefsteak is always good," he offered.

"Oh, damn it all! Don't take that attitude!" Ralph began to show signs of losing his temper again. "This is serious."

"All right. Anybody see this fracas?"

"Yes; that pair of damned nasty old maids next door."

"Well, then, you've got witnesses. If you're aching for vengeance, you can sue Hamilton for assault and battery, and collect damages."

"Is that all?" Ralph was plainly disappointed.

"What did you expect? That he'd be sent up for life?"

"But the fellow didn't only strike me; he threatened to kill me."

"That so? What did he say?"

Ralph decided that it would be inadvisable to quote Whitney's threat verbatim. It had contained such humiliating details as a promise to punch his fat head and to knock his brains out if he had any.

"He simply said that he intended to kill me," he compromised. "And what's more, he sounded as though he meant it."

This time Jefferson didn't suppress the smile.

"If every man who threatened to knock another man's head off actually did it," he said, unwittingly hitting almost upon Whitney's exact words, "practically one half of our male population would be decapitated. If I were you, I'd simply forget about the whole thing."

Ralph set his jaw stubbornly.

"Forget hell!" he exclaimed. "You seem to be taking this whole thing as a huge joke, Carter. But believe me, when a man who's already had one charge of murder against him threatens your life, it's not funny. I demand protection, and it's your duty to see that I get it."

"Suppose you stop beating about the bush and tell me just what it is you want me to do."

"I want you," Ralph stated baldly, "to have Hamilton run out of town as an undesirable and dangerous character."

The district attorney looked his visitor straight in his good eye.

"Are you sure," he asked point blank, "that your fear isn't so much for your own safety as that your grandmother may find out about your affair with Ruth Hamilton?"

Ralph's guilty start betrayed that this shot had struck home, although he tried to cover it up with bluster.

"If that's the attitude you're going to take," he half snarled, "there's no use my talking to you any longer. But I've told you my life is in danger. If anything happens to me, your office will be to blame."

He sprang up and slammed out of the office.

Jefferson stared disgustedly at the still quivering door.

"Oh, go to hell," he muttered under his breath.

7

MURDER

(Wednesday, 2:15 p.m. to Thursday, 2:30 a.m.)

I.

Ronnie ran the tips of her fingers gently along the strip of adhesive tape that decorated Whitney's left cheek.

"I know how you must have felt, Whitney," she said, "and I don't blame you. Still, I—I wish it hadn't happened."

"I don't," he answered recklessly. "Lord, Ronnie! You'll never know what a satisfaction it was to punch his thick head, even if I didn't get the letter."

"Did anyone see you?" she asked.

"Phoebe and Maime were studying the birds again, as usual, so I had to tell them all about it at lunch time. And would you believe it? The old girls actually glowed!"

Ronnie smiled; then her expression sobered.

"If only no one had seen it!" she exclaimed apprehensively. "In case Ralph should decide to do something—"

"What can he do?" he asked.

"He might try to have you arrested. And if he knows the girls saw, he'll drag them in as witnesses."

He shook his head reassuringly.

"There's little danger of that," he said. "He'll know that if he tried it, the whole nasty business would come out, and your grandmother would find out about his connection with Ruth. That's just about the last thing he'd want—oh, good Lord!" he broke off. "Ronnie, I *have* made a mess of things!"

"How do you mean?" she asked, her apprehension returning.

"Like a fool, I've antagonized Ralph now. Suppose he decides to destroy that letter in revenge for the beating I gave him!"

Ronnie's face went white.

"He might do it, at that!" she exclaimed. "Whitney, we've got to get the letter before he thinks of it!"

"Isn't there some legal action we could take?" he asked. "Like having the letter seized as state's evidence?"

"We could do something like that if we applied to have the case reopened," she admitted. "But that would take a long time. We've

44

got to act at once, before it's too late."

"Want me to have another go at him?" he asked hopefully.

"No," she answered. "Let me handle it this time, Whitney."

"You're not going to knuckle down to him, Ronnie. I won't have it!"

"No," she agreed, "I won't do that."

She stared off into the distance where the gaudy colors of sunset were beginning to fade before the approach of night.

"I hate to resort to what amounts practically to blackmail," she said presently, "but I suppose we've got to fight fire with fire. I'm going to tell Ralph that unless he turns that letter over to me, I'm going to Gram with the whole story."

"Suppose he refuses?"

"He won't. Or at least he'll ask for time to think the situation over. And that will give us time, too."

"Ronnie, I don't like your becoming mixed up in this," Whitney declared. "Let me fight my own battle."

She turned to him in the gathering darkness.

"It's my battle, too," she reminded him. "And this is the only way to fight it."

II.

Dr. Richards looked up with a frown as Helen Godwin came into his luxuriously appointed consulting room.

"Now what's wrong?" he demanded irritably.

Helen seated herself in the patient's chair without waiting for an invitation.

"It's that lawyer again," she announced.

"Carter?" The doctor's eyebrows lifted ever so slightly. "I thought we'd dispose of him this morning. Or are you having private misgivings about the old lady's will?"

"It's not the will," Helen answered. "I think he suspects about the hallucinations."

The doctor's indifference vanished.

"How do you know?" he demanded.

"After she'd signed the will," the nurse replied, "she kept him there talking for over half an hour. I couldn't catch all that they said, but I heard her telling him how the ghost ran into my room last night. I managed to interrupt just then, but I'm afraid it was too late. He— he looked as though he'd gotten the idea."

The doctor swore.

"I told you never to go back to your own room!" he snarled savagely. "you had a right to run into the hall or the bathroom, as you always did other times."

"But I couldn't that time," Helen protested. "I'd heard Ronnie's door open almost as soon as the old woman screamed. I'd have run into her if I'd gone into the hall. And somebody had left the light burning in the bathroom. I'd—"

He waved her impatiently to silence.

"Shut up," he said roughly. "I've got to think this thing out."

He rested his bald head between his two hands, massaging the shining scalp with his long, blunt fingers. Helen sat watching him, her own fingers intertwining restlessly in her lap.

At length he looked up.

"We've got to prove to the old lady, and through her to the lawyer, that you've got nothing to do with this," he announced. "Tonight, see that the side door downstairs is left open. I'll come in that way around—say two o'clock, and play ghost myself. You, of course, will be with one of the others at the time to establish your alibi."

"With which one?" Helen asked.

"I'd suggest Ralph. It oughtn't to be difficult for one of your talents."

"Do you take me for a fool?" the girl demanded indignantly.

The doctor smiled.

"That wouldn't have been the word I'd have chosen," he replied. "But we needn't get technical. However, I see your point: If the old lady found out about it, she'd not only ruin your little game with her grandson, but she'd sack you in the bargain; and that would interfere with my own plans. Or wait," he interrupted himself. "I've a better scheme. We're going to take Ralph in on this."

"You mean—tell him you're trying to make it appear that his grandmother is losing her mind?" she demanded incredulously.

"No, of course not," he snapped. "Do you think I'd be fool enough to put myself in the hands of that worthless young pup? You're going to convince him that the old woman is really going insane, and show him how he can get control of his part of the estate by having her put away. Lord!" he exclaimed, his enthusiasm mounting. "Why didn't I think of this long ago!"

"But he can't," Helen pointed out. "If anything happens to Mrs. Marsden, Ronnie becomes his legal guardian so far as the money's concerned."

"He can break that part of the will," the doctor told her. "Tell him that, and it will give him a motive for pulling our chestnuts out of the fire for us. It will also," he added as though it were an afterthought, "give you a reason for seeing him alone tonight."

Helene looked at him thoughtfully.

"It's a wonder," she observed, "that you bother with this sort of chestnuts. You being a doctor, it would be so easy—"

"No!" he cut her short. "Murder is too dangerous. If it was

found out, it would mean the chair; whereas if this goes wrong . . ."

"If this goes wrong, you shrug your shoulders and know nothing," she finished for him, "while I, the scheming adventuress with designs upon the old lady's grandson and his money, take the blame. Well, I've got to take that chance, and you know it; but I'm warning you, Richards, if you try to double-cross me with either Ralph or the old lady, I'll spill the whole thing to her myself—and to that smart lawyer, Steve Carter."

His hand closed, almost without his knowing it, about a bronze letter-opener that lay on the desk. "You keep away from Carter!" he barked at her. "Or by God, I'll—"

"You don't need to worry," she told him; "I'm not going to Carter unless I have to." She rose and started toward the door. "But I'm just warning you, that's all," she flung back.

III.

Ronnie stopped before the door of the room which her cousin Ralph called his den. There was a light visible beneath the bottom of it, so she knew that he must be inside. She raised her hand to knock, then changed her mind and turned the knob, entering unannounced.

"Ralph, I want to talk to you," she said.

Her cousin scowled up at her from the depths of the lounge chair in which he lay rather than sat.

"Well, I don't want to talk to you or to anyone else," he snapped ungraciously. "Get out and leave me alone."

Ronnie didn't move.

"Then you'll listen," she returned calmly, although her heart was pounding wildly. "Ralph, I want that letter."

His frown gradually became a leer.

"So you're ready to talk business now, are you?" he asked. "Well, it's only fair to tell you at the beginning that the price has gone up since last night, sister. Instead of half of Gram's money, I want all of it now—to pay me for what your boy friend did to me this morning. Are you ready to meet the price?"

"No," Ronnie answered, "I'm not; because I can't promise you what isn't mine to give. I don't know what Gram's planning to do with her money—"

"Sez you!"

"—but you're going to turn that letter over to me, just the same," she finished as though he had not interrupted.

He looked at her as though he thought he must have misunderstood.

"Ron, are you crazy?" he asked.

She ignored the question.

"I hate to do this, Ralph," she continued, "but you're forcing me to. Either you'll give me that letter, or I'll go to Gram with the whole story of what's in it."

She saw a look of sudden fear that leaped into his eyes, though he tried to brazen the situation out.

"And what could you hope to gain by that?" he demanded.

"It isn't what I'd gain; it's what you'd lose. Once Gram heard that story, she'd never give you control of your money."

"Why, you—" He cursed viciously. "If you weren't a girl, I'd—" Then an expression of cunning crept into his face. "You do that," he told her, "and I'll burn the letter. Then you'll never be able to clear your precious Whitney's name."

Ronnie felt as though every drop of blood in her body had suddenly rushed back to her heart and become congested there.

"You wouldn't dare!" she gasped.

"Oh, wouldn't I?" He had seen the color recede from her face, and knew that he was now master of the situation. He rose deliberately, crossed to the writing desk and, pulling open one of its drawers, took out Ruth Hamilton's letter. "Since I won't give you this unless you meet my price," he remarked, "and since you threaten to blab on me to Gram if I don't give it to you, it looks as if we'd reached a deadlock, cousin mine. So I might as well get my little job of burning over with right away."

He withdrew a match from the little brass container on the desk and snapped its head with his thumbnail.

"Ralph, no!"

He moved the lighted match with slow deliberation toward the letter.

"Ralph, listen to me." Ronnie was desperate now. "I can't promise you Gram's money, but I'll tell you what I will do: I've still got nearly twenty-five thousand dollars of the money Gramp left me. I'll turn that over to you, and I'll do my best to get Gram's consent to your marrying Helen, if you'll give me that letter."

He paused, with letter and match less than two inches apart.

"You propose to do this when?" he inquired.

"I'll write you a check for the money tonight."

"And stop payment on it at the bank before I can get it cashed."

"No, Ralph; I promise. Or if you'd rather, I'll withdraw the cash money myself and give it to you. You can keep the letter until I do."

He shook out the match, which had begun to scorch his fingers.

"All right, it's a deal," he agreed. "But remember, Ron, no tricks, or the letter goes up in smoke."

Ronnie left the room without answering.

IV.

The ringing of the telephone beside his bed drilled its way into Stephen's sleep-drugged consciousness. Without opening his eyes he reached out automatically and shut off the alarm clock. Then, when the ringing continued, he raised himself upon one elbow and picked up the instrument.

"Hello," he mumbled sleepily into the transmitter. "Now it's your turn."

"Stephen, is that you?" The voice at the other end, tense with excitement but guardedly low-pitched, was Mrs. Marsden's.

"Yes, ma'am." Stephen was wide awake at once. "Is anything wrong?"

"No; that is, not with me. I've simply taken you at your word and called you as soon as I got that picture. At least I think I've got it."

"Well, shut my mouth!" Stephen was sitting up now, all thought of sleep forgotten. "What happened?"

"About twenty minutes ago," Mrs. Marsden began, "I got awake, just as I always do, with the feeling that someone was staring at me. I pretended I was still asleep; but I had the camera you brought me this evening propped under the edge of my pillow with its lens focused on the foot of the bed, and I managed to make three exposures—you told me that the film would turn automatically. One of them, at least, ought to turn out all right."

"Good for you!" Stephen exclaimed with enthusiasm. Then he asked, "What became of the white figure?"

"It stood there for nearly ten minutes waiting for me to notice it," she replied with a chuckle. "It even shook the bed a little, trying to rouse me. But when it saw I wouldn't pay any attention to it, it muttered what sounded like a swear word and went out through the hall door."

"Could you recognize the voice?"

"No, but I think it was a man's. I tried to call you right away, but this blamed line of mine was busy."

"Then it looks like that rules out—" Stephen began, when a sound at the end of the wire cut across his words. It was faint and far away, as though it had occurred at some distance from the other telephone; but it left no doubt as to its nature. It had been the unmistakable report of a shot!

"Mrs. Marsden, what's happened?" Stephen shouted, but he received no answer.

However, he could tell that the connection had not been broken, for distant sounds continued to reach him. He pressed the receiver tight against his ear, trying to distinguish what they were.

There were running footsteps, the slamming of a door, then the sound of excited voices. Among the latter he thought he recognized old Mrs. Marsden's but he couldn't be sure.

"Mrs. Marsden!" he called again. "Are you all right? What's happened?"

Still he received no answer.

The door to his room opened, and Jefferson appeared in his pajamas.

"What the devil's going on in here?" he demanded.

"I don't know yet," Stephen answered. "I was talking to Mrs. Marsden, when there came what sounded like a shot—"

Jefferson crossed the room in a single stride and snatched the telephone.

"Hello!" be bellowed into the transmitter. "What's happened there? Somebody answer this phone!"

He continued to shout until he finally got a reply.

Watching him, Stephen saw an expression of almost incredulous astonishment leap into his face.

"Good Lord!" Jefferson exclaimed; then, in clipped, businesslike tones: "Warn everybody not to touch anything. I'll be there at once."

He jammed the telephone back upon its cradle only long enough to sever the connection, then picked it up again.

"Get into your clothes, Steve, while I call the homicide bureau," he commanded as he dialed a number. "Ralph Marsden has just been murdered!"

8

INVESTIGATION

(Thursday, 3 a.m. to 4 a.m.)

I.

The front door of the Marsden house was opened to Stephen and Jefferson by Detective Donovan of the city homicide bureau.

"The body's upstairs in a little room they call the den, Mr. Carter," he said in response to Jefferson's question. "The old lady, her granddaughter an' a trained nurse are all in the old lady's bedroom. We only just got here ourselves, so we ain't had time to question them yet."

"I'll attend to that," Jefferson said. He started toward the stairs with Stephen at his heels, but the detective had something else to tell him.

"An' guess who else is here, Mr. Carter?" he called after him. "You remember that Pittsburgh case about—"

"Yes, I know," Jefferson interrupted him. "Albert Hamilton."

"Well, shut my mouth!" Stephen exclaimed, while the detective at the foot of the stairs muttered something more forceful. "How'd you find out about Hamilton, Jeff?"

"Tell you later," Jefferson answered. "Just now we've got other things to attend to."

When they reached the top of the stairs, Jefferson started in the direction of Mrs. Marsden's room; then, apparently changing his mind, he turned and continued on down the hall to a room where a light was burning.

Detective Sergeant Forbes, from the district attorney's staff, and Coroner Lufkin were in the room. The coroner was bending over Ralph Marsden's body, which lay crumpled on the floor midway between the door and a big lounge chair.

"Shot through the heart," he announced, rising. "And at close range, too. The front of his shirt's actually scorched from the flash. It must have happened less than half an hour ago."

"It did," Jefferson affirmed. "Steve was talking to old Mrs. Marsden, and heard the shot over the telephone." He crossed to the body and stood looking down at it. "Find the gun?" he asked.

"No," the coroner answered. "The murderer had the foresight to

51

take it away with him. But it must have been a young cannon," he added, "judging by the hole it made in Marsden."

Sergeant Forbes spoke.

"We know how the murderer got in and out, Mr. Carter," he volunteered. "The back stairway comes up just next to this room, and there's a door almost at its foot that opens onto the side porch. That door wasn't only unlocked, but it was standing wide open. Want to see it?"

"Not now," Jefferson answered. "It can wait until I've talked to the family. You've put the fingerprint boys on it, I suppose?"

"They haven't got here yet," Forbes replied, "but—that must be them now," he interrupted himself as there sounded a loud ring at the front doorbell. "I'll go down and put them to work."

He hurried toward the stairs, while Jefferson and Stephen moved off in the direction of Mrs. Marsden's room, leaving the coroner to complete his examination of the body alone.

Mrs. Marsden was sitting up in bed. She was wearing a quilted bed jacket over her nightgown. Ronnie, with Whitney Hamilton standing beside her, was sitting in a chair near the bed. The nurse was nowhere in sight.

"Mrs. Marsden, I can't tell you how sorry I am—" Jefferson began, but she interrupted him.

"You can skip all that, Jefferson," she told him. "Ralph wasn't any good in life, and you know it, so there's no use your pretending that you thought he was now that he's dead. But he was my grandson"—there was a momentary quivering of the muscles of the old face—"and I want his murderer found and punished. Now what do you want us to tell you?"

Jefferson looked somewhat disconcerted. Although he had known Mrs. Marsden for nearly ten years, she had never ceased to be a source of surprise to him.

"Well, first of all," he said, trying to speak as impersonally as possible, "I'd like you to tell me, Mrs. Marsden, whether you know of any enemies that Ralph had. Serious ones, I mean, who may have hated him sufficiently to take his life."

"No," she answered at once, "I don't know of anybody like that. Ralph was always his own worst enemy."

The district attorney wondered whether that was strictly true. Men like Ralph Marsden, he knew, often formed deep and bitter enmities which they themselves never suspected. However, he let the point pass.

"Who was it discovered the—your grandson?" he asked.

"I think I can answer that, Mr. Carter," Ronnie spoke up. "I was in my room when I heard the—the shot. I ran out into the hall at about the same time that Helen Godwin, Gram's nurse, opened the door. I asked her what had happened, and she said she didn't know. Then we both saw the open door of the den, and what looked like a cloud of smoke in the lighted room beyond. We ran down the hall together, and found Ralph."

"How long was it between the time that you heard the shot and the time you noticed the light in the den?" Jefferson asked.

Ronnie considered.

"It may have been as long as a minute," she replied. "You know how it is when you hear a sound like that in the middle of the night; you're sort of stunned by it for the first couple of seconds."

The district attorney nodded.

"Then you didn't see anyone leaving the den?" he inquired.

She shook her head.

"Or hear anyone run down those back stairs?"

"No," she answered. "At least I didn't. I can't say for Helen."

"Where is Miss Godwin now?"

Mrs. Marsden intervened.

"She was feeling pretty badly over what had happened," she explained, "so I told her she should go to her room and lie down. She was rather fond of Ralph," she added.

Jefferson turned back to Ronnie.

"Did either you or Miss Godwin touch Ralph?" he asked.

"Helen did, being a nurse," she replied. "I wanted to send for Dr. Richards; but she said it wouldn't be any use, that Ralph was already dead. Then I went to tell Gram what had happened."

"And Miss Godwin . . . ?"

"Stayed with Ralph, I think."

"I'd like to question her later," the district attorney remarked, "but we'll let her go for the present. Who else sleeps in the house?"

"No one else. The cook and the parlor maid both live out."

Jefferson turned upon Whitney.

"How do you happen to be here, Hamilton?" he demanded.

"I came over as soon as I heard the shot," Whitney replied. He did not seem surprised that the district attorney should have known his name. "I was afraid something had happened to Ronnie."

"Why Ronnie particularly?"

Whitney hesitated, then he replied:

"Ronnie and I have just become engaged to be married. It was only natural that I should have thought of her first."

"I see. But you stopped to dress before you came?"

"No; I was already dressed. I hadn't gone to bed yet."

"At half past two in the morning?"

"At half past two in the morning," Whitney repeated simply, and offered no explanation.

Jefferson let the matter pass, and put another question.

"How did you get into this house? Did you ring for somebody to come and let you in?"

"No," Whitney answered. "The side door was standing open, so I came in that way. Ronnie met me in the upper hall—I'd called her name as I came up the back stairs—and told me that Ralph had been shot."

"Did you see anyone leaving the house by that side door just before you reached it?"

"No, I did not."

"But you would have seen anyone who might have gone that way, wouldn't you?"

"Not necessarily. He could have gone out while I was running down the stairs from my room in the house next door. Besides, it was dark over here on the porch."

"But not too dark for you to notice the open door, and make straight for it?"

Of a sudden Whitney seemed to realize where the district attorney's questions were leading, for there leaped into his eyes the stricken look of a hunted animal that has once felt the trap, and now sees its steel jaws about to close upon him a second time.

"I didn't know the door was open until I reached it," he declared, but the note of desperation in his voice robbed it of convincingness. "I headed for it simply because it was the nearest—"

Old Mrs. Marsden's voice cut across his words.

"Never mind, Whitney," she interrupted him; then to Jefferson, "Jeff Carter, that'll do. Don't think that because this boy was unfortunate enough to have been innocently involved in a murder case once before you're going to victimize him a second time; I won't have it. If you want to know whether anybody left this house by the side door tonight, why don't you go talk to the Heisy girls and find out what they can tell you? If Maime Heisy didn't see this person leave and can't tell you who he was and all about him, then she's losing her grip."

Jefferson looked annoyed; then a slow grin overspread his face.

"Maybe that's not such a bad idea at that," he observed. "Come on, Steve; I think we'll try it."

II.

The two Heisy girls sat side by side on the sofa in their living room. They were both fully clothed, and had the air of having been expecting their visitors, or at least some members of the city's law enforcement agencies.

"Yes, Mr. District Attorney," Miss Maime was saying importantly, "we can tell you all about it. We heard The Shot." She capitalized it with her voice, making it sound, Stephen thought, as though it had been the Crack of Doom.

Jefferson looked decidedly interested.

"Were you awake when you heard it, Miss Heisy," he asked, "or did it waken you?"

"It woke me, of course," Miss Maime answered in a tone which implied that she would have considered it vaguely indecent to have been awake at that hour. "At first I thought it must have been the backfire from an automobile; then I remembered that there aren't many cars on the streets so late at night any more, what with the gasoline rationing and the rubber shortage and all. So I sat up in bed and I said to Phoebe, 'That sounded like a shot,' and—" She broke off in sudden confusion. "But I guess you don't care about that part, do you?" she asked.

Jefferson tried not to show his pleased surprise at this unexpected offer of a curtailment. He had met Miss Maime Heisy on several occasions before—not, however, in connection with his official capacity—and he had been prepared for a long and detailed account of what "I said" and what "our Phoebe said" and what "our mom and our pop used to say."

"You don't need to bother going into details," he told her diplomatically. "If you'll just tell me what you saw and heard. . . ."

Miss Maime took the hint.

"Well," she began, "after I said how it must have been a shot, I got up and went over to the window to look out. But I didn't see anything or anybody down on the street. Then I glanced toward the Marsden house—my sister and I share the corner room—and I saw that there was a light in one of the back rooms upstairs. I thought maybe somebody was sick, or that Mary Marsden had had one of her spells; and I was just wondering whether I ought to phone over there and ask if there was anything I could do, when I saw—The Man."

"You saw a man come out of the Marsden house?" In his eagerness Jefferson leaned forward unwarily, and almost skidded off the treacherous horsehair chair onto the floor.

Miss Maime nodded, the tightly screwed knob of hair on the top of her head seeming to curtsy with the gesture.

"He came out that side door," she declared; "the one that opens near the foot of the back stairs onto the side porch. It was so dark over there, I couldn't have seen him at all if he hadn't been wearing white."

"You're right sure it was a man?" Stephen put in.

"Oh, yes." Miss Maime was positive. "At first, though, I thought it was That Nurse." The way she pronounced the "that" made it a one-word summary of her opinion of Helen Godwin. "Then he started to run across the garden, and I saw that he was wearing

trousers instead of a skirt. Then he disappeared under the trees beside
the tennis court, and after that I couldn't see him any more."

"Miss Heisy, please think carefully," Jefferson directed. "Did this
man look like anyone you know, or was there anything even vaguely
familiar about him?"

Miss Maime looked as though she would have liked to oblige with
a full and detailed description, but couldn't without straining both
her conscience and the truth.

"No," she said regretfully, "although I sort of took for granted
at the time that it was Ralph, and I wondered whether Mary Marsden
had been taken particularly bad. I thought it was funny that if they
needed a doctor, they didn't telephone instead of—Oh!" The exclama-
tion was a cross between a screech and a squawk. "That man must
have been the—the murderer!"

"We've every reason so far to think so," Jefferson agreed gravely.
"But you say you thought at first that he was Ralph Marsden. Was
he about Ralph's size?"

"Well, no," Miss Maime admitted. "He was smaller—thinner, that
is. I couldn't tell how tall he was, because he was bending over as he
ran. I merely thought it might be Ralph because he was the only
man over there."

Jefferson turned abruptly to a new topic.

"Miss Heisy," he inquired, "did you see or hear your boarder, Mr.
Hamilton, go out after the shot was fired?"

"Whitney isn't just a boarder," Miss Phoebe broke in defensively,
speaking for the first time. "He's like our own—like one of the
family."

"Hush, Phoebe," Miss Maime said aside. "That isn't what Mr.
Carter wants to know." Then to the district attorney, "Yes, I heard
him on the stairs, so I called out to him and asked him if he was
going over to the Marsden's to see what was wrong there. He said
he was, so I told him to telephone back and let us know, and he
promised he would. Only he must have forgotten, for I had to call
up myself and ask. That's how we happened to know about Ralph,"
she added explanatorily.

"And this was before or after you saw the man leaving the Marsden house?"

"Right afterwards. I remember because I was listening to see if
Ralph—I still thought that that was who it was—might be coming
over here to call us, and I wondered—"

"Are you sure"—Jefferson could not restrain himself from interrupting what promised to be a detour into Miss Maime's mental processes—"that when you heard Mr. Hamilton on the stairs, he wasn't
coming up instead of going down?"

She looked at him as though she suspected him of not being over-strong in his intellect.

"Seeing that he was on his way out of the house, he had to be going down," she replied with a touch of tartness. "The boy isn't a parachute jumper."

"No, of course not," Jefferson said, rising. "Well, I don't think we need bother you and your sister further, Miss Heisy. Thank you very much for your information."

When their visitors had gone, Miss Phoebe turned upon her sister.

"Maime," she demanded with a fierceness unusual in her, "why in the world did you have to tell about—about seeing that man?"

"Well, I did see a man," Miss Maime said defensively, "so why shouldn't I have told?"

"Maybe you did," Miss Phoebe admitted "but have you always got to tell everything you know? Don't you realize what that district attorney thinks?" she flung out in desperation. "He thinks it was Whitney!"

9

INFORMATION

I.

The glare of a photo flash bulb told Stephen and Jefferson, as they mounted the stairs to the second floor of the Marsden house, that the fingerprint men and photographers were at work in the den. The district attorney walked down the hall to the open door.

"Turn up anything so far?" he inquired of Sergeant Forbes, who was supervising operations.

"Not yet," the detective answered. "That door downstairs was a washout. Whoever went through it last wiped both knobs clean. The boys haven't finished in here yet"—he gestured toward the interior of the room—"but so far they've turned up so many different prints, I doubt if any of them will do us any good."

"I was afraid of that," Jefferson remarked. "Have you printed that crowd back there yet?" He jerked his head in the direction of Mrs. Marsden's bedroom.

"Donovan attended to that," Forbes replied. "And that reminds me, Mr. Carter: The nurse said she wanted to talk to you when you came back. She wouldn't tell Donovan and me what it was about."

"Good!" Jefferson exclaimed. "I was about to send for her anyway. Go get her, Forbes, and bring her"—he glanced around the hall—"bring her in here." He opened the door to what had been Ralph Marsden's bedroom.

"What you guess she wants to tell you, Jeff?" Stephen inquired while they waited.

"I haven't the faintest idea," Jefferson replied. Then he asked suspiciously, "Have you?"

Stephen smiled.

"I've kind of a notion," he answered, "that she wants to confess. Oh, not to the murder," as he saw his brother's expression of incredulity; "to something else. I'll explain to you later if I'm right."

"You'll explain to me in any case," Jefferson began; but just then the door opened, and Forbes entered with Helen Godwin.

The nurse looked excited, but there were not, Stephen observed, any noticeable signs of grief in her face such as Mrs. Marsden's state-

58

ment about her earlier had led him to suspect. He wondered whether she had feigned emotion to the old lady as a pretext to be alone for reasons best known to herself.

"This is Nurse Godwin, Mr. Carter," the sergeant announced.

The district attorney pushed a chair forward for her.

"Please sit here, Miss—" he began, and stopped. "Godwin?" he repeated, staring at her keenly. "Weren't you the nurse in charge of that patient who died from an overdose of morphine about two years ago?"

Helen stiffened.

"It was proved that I had nothing to do with that," she retorted resentfully. "The patient got hold of the tablets himself, and took an overdose. But if you're going to drag that out and start holding it against me now—"

"I'm not holding anything against you, Miss Godwin," Jefferson told her. "The fact that you were accused of a so-called mercy killing once is no indication, to my mind at least, that you may have had anything to do with the present case."

"Liar," Stephen muttered under his breath, remembering his brother's recent line of questioning of Whitney Hamilton. But he looked at the nurse with new interest. If Dr. Richards had been the attendant physician in the case Jefferson had just mentioned, it might have some possible significance.

"Now, Miss Godwin," Jefferson inquired when the nurse, somewhat mollified, had seated herself, "what is it you have to tell me?"

Helen hesitated, while her hand fumbled with something in the pocket of her uniform. Then she raised her eyes boldly to the district attorney's face.

"I know who killed Ralph Marsden," she announced.

"You—what?" Jefferson actually jumped. Stephen, too, was taken by surprise. This was something he had not been expecting.

Helen brought her hand out of her uniform pocket. She was holding a folded and slightly crumpled letter.

"Here, read this," she directed, and extended it toward him.

Jefferson took the single sheet of paper, unfolded it and, with Stephen reading around his arm, ran quickly through it.

"Good Lord!" he exclaimed as soon as he had finished. "Why, this amounts practically to a confession of a murder that must have been committed"—he consulted the date in the heading of the letter—"nearly a year ago! Where did you get this, Miss Godwin?"

"Ralph had it clutched in his hand when we found him," Helen answered. "I suppose I shouldn't have touched it, but I did it without thinking. Then when I saw what it was, I decided I'd better keep it so that nobody else could get hold of it and destroy it."

He didn't rebuke her for her action.

"You're suggesting that the woman who wrote this killed Marsden to get it back?"

"No," she answered. "She died the day after she wrote it; got her cups mixed, and drank her own poison by mistake." She paused; then she added meaningfully, "Her name was Ruth Hamilton."

"Good Lord above!" In his excitement Jefferson half rose from his chair. Then he sat down again, slowly.

"Tell me, Miss Godwin," he said: "to your definite knowledge, was Albert Hamilton aware that Marsden had this letter?"

At first the name puzzled her; then she realized to whom he was referring.

"Yes," she answered. "To my definite knowledge, he was."

She glanced away for an instant; then she brought her eyes back to the district attorney's face.

"I'm going to tell you everything I know, Mr. Carter," she declared, "and you can make of it whatever you see fit.

"For the past month or so, Ralph Marsden and I have wanted to get married; but he was afraid he couldn't get his grandmother's consent. I felt that we might be able to handle the old lady if it wasn't for Ronnie Marsden—she's always looked down on me as being beneath her—and night before last, I told Ralph so. He said that if I was sure that was the case, he knew how he could make Ronnie stop interfering with us fast enough. Not only that, but he said he could make her actually help us, and be glad for the chance."

"He meant by offering her this letter that would clear Hamilton of suspicion in his wife's death, in exchange for her help?" Jefferson asked.

Helen nodded.

"Although I didn't know that at the time," she amended. "Then that night when Ronnie came home, Ralph made her his proposition. But she wouldn't give him a definite answer."

"But why, Miss Godwin?" Stephen put in. "I'd have thought Miss Ronnie would have been right anxious to help Mr. Hamilton clear his name."

Helen shot him an annoyed glance, then lowered her eyes before his steady gaze.

"I—I think Ralph wanted a cash settlement or something included in the deal," she admitted reluctantly, "and Ronnie either couldn't or wouldn't agree to it. But she must have run to Whitney Hamilton with the whole thing as soon as she got a chance; for the next morning he came over here, called Ralph outside and demanded the letter. When Ralph wouldn't give it to him, Whitney threatened to kill him; and as a matter of fact, he did beat him almost into unconsciousness. But he didn't get the letter."

"Apparently not," Jefferson observed, glancing down at the letter, which he still held in his hand. "So you think he came back tonight to get it?"

"He must have," Helen declared. "I talked to Ralph earlier this evening"—she was careful not to mention the time—"and he told me that Ronnie had arranged with him to pay twenty-five thousand dollars for the letter in the morning. But that was just talk to put Ralph off his guard. Anyway, a little after two o'clock this morning, I heard Ralph's private telephone in the den ring. Whitney Hamilton must have called him up and asked to see him, then come over here and shot him in an attempt to get the letter."

"'Must have' isn't 'it,'" Stephen interrupted again. "Besides, if that was what happened, Miss Godwin, why didn't Hamilton take the letter away with him?"

This time the look she cast in his direction was one of downright hostility, but she had an answer ready.

"Because he didn't have time," she flung at him. "He had to get away before the sound of the shot brought everybody running. Then, besides, he was probably counting on Ronnie's finding the letter. It was just luck that I happened to see it first, while she went to tell her grandmother what had happened."

"A good point," Jefferson approved. He remained deep in thought for the space of nearly a minute; then, realizing that anything she might add to her story would only be surmise, he rose and opened the door for her, signifying that the interview was at an end.

"Thank you for telling us all this, Miss Godwin," he said. "I'll treat it confidentially, of course; and I'd advise you not to repeat it to anyone else for the present."

"With a killer loose on the premises, I'm not likely to," Helen observed, and left the room.

II.

Detective Sergeant Forbes, who at a nod from the district attorney had remained present during the interview, dropped weakly into the nearest chair, mopping his broad forehead with his handkerchief.

"My God!" he muttered. "Imagine a guy tryin' to clear himself of one murder by committin' another!"

Jefferson nodded.

"It doesn't make much sense, does it?" he asked.

"That's just the point!" Stephen broke in excitedly. "It doesn't make *any* sense. Whitney Hamilton didn't have to establish his innocence of his wife's death; he'd already been cleared of that charge legally. That shows he wanted the case cleared up only so he could feel free to marry Miss Ronnie without the suspicion of an unsolved crime hanging over him. Would a man who felt that way about a girl be likely to commit murder, when that was the very thing he wanted to clear himself of for her sake? And besides, having barely gotten off once when he was innocent, would he be likely to put his neck in danger a second time by actually doing the thing he'd been charged with the first time? Of course he wouldn't."

Jefferson heaved a sigh of tolerant resignation.

"Steve, I've never known it to fail," he said. "As soon as I pick out a likely suspect in a murder case, you fly at once to his defense. But this time I'm afraid you're wrong. So far as we know, Hamilton was the only person with a motive for killing Ralph Marsden."

"So far as we know." Stephen pounced upon the phrase. "But what makes you think we know it all, Jeff? And what about that telephone call the nurse says Ralph received around two o'clock in the morning? She's only surmising that it was Hamilton who called. But anyway, you'll need more than just a motive to build a case against him; you'll need evidence. And all you've got is that girl's unsupported word."

"I'm not putting much faith in that telephone call, either way," Jefferson informed him. "I think she invented that detail out of whole cloth, so as not to appear to have been the last person who had talked to Ralph before he was killed. But as to my having nothing but her unsupported word in a case against Hamilton, I've got a little more than that. Yesterday afternoon Ralph Marsden came into my office and told me all about the fight they'd had. He accused Hamilton then of having designs upon his life."

"You can't use that in court," Stephen shot back. "The accusation of a dead man can't be admitted in evidence unless the man was dying at the time he made it, and knew he was dying. That's the law."

"Thanks; so I've heard," Jefferson remarked dryly, while the sergeant concealed a grin behind his broad palm. "But it so happens that there were witnesses to that fight; and if they overheard Hamilton threaten to kill Ralph, that'll be admissible as evidence in any man's court."

"Witnesses?" Stephen repeated, as though he doubted it. "Who?"

"Our old friends, the Heisy girls." Jefferson turned to Sergeant Forbes. "And there's something for you to do, Forbes," he said. "Go around and question the Heisys first thing tomorrow morning—their house is the one next to this one on the upper side—and find out just how much they know about that fight. You'll have to be pretty diplomatic about it, for I got the impression when I was over there a while ago that they're pretty fond of Hamilton; and they'll probably close up like clams if they get the idea that anything they say might react against him."

"Jeff," Stephen inquired, "don't you ever hate yourself?"

"Lord, yes!" Jefferson admitted wearily. "And it looks as though this were going to be one of the times. Don't think I'm going to enjoy prosecuting that poor devil, Steve, or making Ronnie Marsden testify against the man she wants to marry, for I'm not. But if he's committed murder, then it's my sworn duty to do everything in my power to see that he gets convicted, regardless of what my own private feelings in the case may be."

"Suppose I can prove that he didn't do it?" Stephen asked.

"If you can do that," Jefferson told him, "you're more than welcome to try."

"That's all I wanted to know!" Stephen exclaimed, and started toward the door.

"Come back here!" the district attorney called after him. "Where do you think you're going?"

Stephen paused in the doorway.

"Just keep your shirt on," he advised. "I'm not going to tip Hamilton off that you're after him, if that's what you're afraid of. I'm only going to see Mrs. Marsden about—about the matter she called me up for tonight in the first place."

He hurried from the room before his brother could delay him with any further questions.

Sergeant Forbes looked after him with interest.

"Now what do you suppose he's up to, Mr. Carter?" he inquired.

Jefferson shook his head in complete bafflement.

"God knows"—he said—"I hope."

10

APPREHENSION

(Thursday, 9:30 a.m. to 10:50 a.m.)

I.

The coroner tossed a little cardboard pillbox across the desk to the district attorney.

"Bullet that killed youg Marsden," he announced. "Looks like a lead slug you could use in a telephone if it was a little flatter."

Jefferson picked up the little box and examined the lead pellet that reposed inside on a dab of cotton wool.

"Good Lord!" he exclaimed. "You said last night that it must have been a young cannon that shot him, and it looks as if you weren't far wrong. Got any idea what sort of gun fires bullets like this?"

The coroner shrugged.

"I'm no expert on the subject," he replied, "but I'd say offhand that it was an old-fashioned army pistol; the kind that was used back during the Spanish-American War and before. The thing tore a hole as big as the end of your little finger straight through his heart and flattened itself against the back of one of his ribs," he went on, referring to the bullet. "I had the devil's own time getting it out."

Jefferson replaced the cover upon the box.

"I'll send it down to the ballistics department and find out what they can tell me about it," he said. "If we can trace a gun like that to Hamilton we'll have him; but I guess there'll be no such luck."

"You think Hamilton did it?" the coroner inquired with interest.

Jefferson nodded.

"I'm afraid so," he replied. "He had motive and opportunity, although so far I haven't been able to get hold of anything to connect him directly with the scene of the crime. Of course, if we have any luck with the gun, it'll be another story."

"A shame he lost his head this time, after being cleared in that other mess," the coroner commented. "But that's the way it goes. Well, I must be getting along." He rose from the corner of the desk where he had been half sitting. "Tomorrow morning suit you all right for the inquest?" he inquired.

"Tomorrow morning's okay," Jefferson affirmed.

As the coroner left the office Detective Sergeant Forbes came in.

64

He looked slightly dizzy.

"I've just taken care of that assignment you gave me last night, Mr. Carter," he announced, dropping into the chair facing the district attorney. "Lord, how that one woman can talk!"

"I should have warned you," Jefferson said with a grin. "Maime Heisy has more strength in her tongue than Joe Louis has in his right arm. Did you find out anything?"

The sergeant grinned faintly in response.

"I think," he replied, "that the murder was committed by 'our pap.' " Then he added more seriously, "Both women admitted having seen the fight. In fact, they seemed downright proud of the shiner Hamilton planted on Marsden, who, according to the tall, skinny one, they 'didn't have much time for.' Then the little one must have caught on to what I was after, for she shut up tighter than a drum. Somehow—although I'm damned if I know how—she managed to tip the other one off; and after that I couldn't get a word out of either of them. That is," he amended, "not a word on what I wanted, although I'm positive they know something."

"Think I could break them down on the witness stand?" Jefferson asked.

Forbes raised one shoulder noncommittaly.

"I'd hate to have your job trying," he said. "Those two old maids are ready to fight tooth and nail for Hamilton—literally, too, I suspect."

The district attorney frowned.

"Then that means we'll never be able to get Miss Maime to identify Hamilton, as the man she saw leaving the Marsden house last night," he said. "But there's one thing she can't back down on: She admitted to Steve and me that the man she saw was dressed in white; and I noticed that Hamilton was wearing a white suit."

"Speaking of Mr. Stephen," Forbes asked, "has he told you yet what he's got up his sleeve?"

"Not yet," Jefferson admitted; "but he promised to come in here this morning with what he called 'some startling new developments.' That's why I didn't have Hamilton and Ronnie Marsden in on the carpet about that letter last night; I thought I'd better wait and see what Steve's up to first. And by the way, Forbes, I'm a little sorry you let the papers have that story about Maime Heisy and what she saw, just in case Hamilton *wasn't* the murderer after all."

"Lord! I never thought of that!" the detective exclaimed, abashed. "Maybe I'd better send a man out there to stick around and keep an eye on her."

"Not a bad idea," Jefferson approved. "And if you've no line of your own that you want to follow right away, you might call the Pittsburgh police long distance and find out whether Hamilton owned a gun at the time he was arrested out there last year; and if he did, what became of it after he was acquitted. Then I wish you'd take this slug down to the ballistics department and find out what they can tell you about the make of gun that fired it." He pushed the little cardboard box across the desk. "It's the bullet that killed Ralph Marsden," he added by way of explanation.

II.

Miss Phoebe laid aside her knitting and glanced at her sister, who was standing with her back to the center of the room, looking out through the crack between the lace curtains.

"Maime," she announced, "I'm worried."

"You mean about the detective that was here a while ago?" Miss Maime asked without turning around. "Well, I didn't tell him anything, did I?"

"No," Miss Phoebe admitted, answering the question in the sense in which it had been put. "But after what you told Mr. Carter and his brother last night about seeing that man . . . Maime, I know they suspect Whitney of killing Ralph Marsden."

"Nonsense!" Miss Maime retorted. "Or anyway, what if they do? They can't prove he did it when he didn't."

Miss Phoebe smiled with the disillusionment of superior wisdom.

"You're no child, Maime,' she pronounced. "You're old enough to know it doesn't always work out that way."

Miss Maime bridled.

"I'm only three years older than you are, Phoebe," she reminded her sister tartly.

"Well, I know it," Miss Phoebe retorted, "so that's all the more reason why you should."

"Fiddlesticks!" Miss Maime pronounced. It was the way she generally settled arguments with Miss Phoebe.

She continued to peer out of the window for a minute or so longer; then she crossed to the old-fashioned secretary-desk that stood in one corner of the room and took from its top drawer the pair of opera glasses. Recrossing to her post by the window, she focused them through the mesh of the lace curtains.

"What do you see, Maime?" Miss Phoebe inquired, half in hope, half in fear.

Miss Maime didn't answer at once. Presently she said:

"Phoebe, come here."

Miss Phoebe crossed to her sister's side.

"What is it?" she asked nervously.

Miss Maime thrust the opera glasses into her hand.

"Take a look at that man across the street there," she commanded.

"Tell me if you think you've ever seen him before."

Miss Phoebe raised the glasses to her own eyes.

"Why," she exclaimed almost at once, "he looks like one of those detectives that was at the Marsdens' last night!"

"I thought so," Miss Maime said. "Phoebe, he's been watching this house for the past fifteen minutes!"

The sisters stared at each other aghast.

III.

Helen Godwin opened the door to Dr. Richards' private consulting room. She walked purposefully across the pool of dappled morning sunlight that had found its way in through the partly open slats of the venetian blinds, to the broad-topped, polished walnut desk behind which the doctor was seated.

"So you were there after all last night," she said levelly.

He stared up at her with a look of truculent defiance.

"Of course I was there," he snapped, interpreting by instinct what she meant. "It wasn't my fault that the old fool wouldn't wake up: I did everything but shake her. But under the circumstances." he added, "it may be just as well that she didn't."

"Yes, it may be—for her," Helen agreed. "She might have recognized you, instead of poor Ralph."

"What do you mean by that?" He made as if to rise from his chair.

"I mean," Helen retorted, unflinching, "that Ralph opened the door to the den on you just as you were passing in the hall, and you shot him to save your own rotten skin."

"Don't be a fool," he said coldly. "I've told you before that I wouldn't go in for murder; it's too dangerous."

"You might have changed your mind when it came to saving yourself from a long term in the penitentiary. Frightening old ladies—especially rich old ladies with weak hearts—is a criminal offense, you know."

He started to form a reply; then a look of sudden cunning crept into his eyes.

"It seems to me," he said instead, "that the arrangement was for you to be with Ralph Marsden at the time of my visit, in order to prove to the old woman and that smart lawyer of hers that you could have had nothing to do with the 'hallucinations.' That makes it look as though you might have shot him."

The nurse laughed derisively.

"Kill the one man who was offering me a decent chance at all the things I've always wanted out of life?" she asked. "Do you think I'm crazy?"

"Then where were you if you weren't with him?" he persisted.

"I was with him until five after two," she replied. "Then some-body rang him up on the telephone—he's got his own private line there in the den—and he told me I'd better clear out; that he was going to have a visitor who might get the wrong idea if I was there with him."

The doctor looked momentarily interested; then his interest gave place to skepticism.

"That's a little too thin," he said. "I was in the house by two o'clock, and I didn't hear any telephone ring."

"You wouldn't have," Helen told him. "The bell's muffled."

He thought for a moment; then he asked:

"If you weren't with Ralph at two-thirty, where were you?"

"I was in my room, next to Mrs. Marsden's."

"You didn't hang around to see who Ralph's visitor might be?"

"Why should I? It was none of my concern."

"It could have occurred to you that it might be another woman."

Her eyes flickered at that. He saw it, and smiled with satisfaction.

"I don't know why you've come here, Miss Godwin," he said. "Probably to extort money out of me, since you can no longer look forward to stepping into a fortune by marrying Ralph Marsden. So I'm warning you right now that if you try it, I'll send an anonymous letter to the police, informing them that you killed Marsden in a jealous rage over another woman. I'm not so sure," he added slyly, "but what that isn't the real truth, after all."

"You do that," she flung back at him, "and I'll tell the D. A. who the man was the Heisy woman saw leaving the house by the side door last night."

"What's that?" He had stiffened to attention.

It was Helen's turn to smile.

"You didn't know about that, did you?" she observed. "Well, read this."

She took a folded newspaper from under her arm and flung it out upon the desk in front of him.

He glanced down at the banner headlines.

" 'Neighbor Sees Murderer Flee—' " he began to read aloud. "Good God! I didn't know that damned old maid had seen me!"

"Is that a confession?" Helen inquired.

"No!" he denied with vigor. "I didn't kill Ralph Marsden. I'll admit I hung around for a while after I'd been in to see the old lady, wondering whether I ought to make a second try. But I finally de-cided against it; and I was halfway down the back stairs on my way out when the shot was fired. I didn't even know what had happened until I heard the announcement on the news broadcast over the radio while I was eating breakfast this morning."

"Crime with your coffee," Helen observed flippantly. "Well, that's all I wanted to know." She turned to leave; then she added, with a sudden change of both tone and manner: "But if I find out you've lied to me, as heaven is my witness, I'll come back and kill you!"

The doctor watched her in silence as she left the office. He waited until he had heard the outer door open and close; then he picked up the telephone and dialed a number.

"I want to speak to Miss Phoebe Heisy," he said when he had gotten his connection. . . .

11

CONFESSION

(Thursday, 10:30 a.m. to 10:50 a.m.)

I.

Miss Phoebe sat down upon the front edge of the chair facing the district attorney, and clutched her big knitting bag in both hands as though she were afraid it would develop a will of its own and try to get away from her. She swallowed once or twice, moistened her pale lips with the tip of her tongue, then announced in a small, frightened voice:

"Mr. Carter, I—I've come to confess."

"Confess?" Jefferson was even more puzzled by the statement than he had been by his caller's arrival a moment before. "Confess what, Miss Phoebe?"

"I mean," Miss Phoebe explained, speaking more firmly this time, "that I've come to confess to the murder of Ralph Marsden."

"The murder of—*what!*" Jefferson almost swallowed his cigar in sheer amazement. "Would you mind saying that again, please?"

Miss Phoebe obliged.

"I shot and killed Ralph Marsden," she repeated patiently, like a school teacher explaining a difficult lesson to a none-too-bright child. "It's rather a long story, Mr. Carter. Would you like me to tell it to you?"

"I would," Jefferson answered with feeling.

"It was this way," the little old lady began, clutching the knitting bag even tighter. "A couple of days ago Mary Marsden—Mrs. Leland Marsden, I mean—had your brother, Stephen, draw up a will for her, leaving all her money and property to Whitney Hamilton. She did this because she knew that Whitney and Ronnie—that's her niece, Veronica—wanted to get married; and she thought that Whitney was afraid to ask her—Ronnie, I mean—for fear it would look as though he was after the Marsden money—you know how men are about such things. And so she—I mean Mrs. Marsden—decided that if she left the money to him instead, not telling him, of course, but just letting him find out that Ronnie wasn't to inherit, he wouldn't feel that way any more; and yet Ronnie would have what she wanted her to have, because when two people are married, what belongs to

70

one belongs to the other.

"She even sent your brother over to our house to tell us all this; not mentioning Whitney, naturally, but just pretending he wanted to know whether we thought Mary Marsden realized what she was doing in making a will that would disinherit her own flesh and blood. But Maime and I saw through it all right away. Your brother is a rather transparent young man, Mr. Carter."

Jefferson suppressed a smile at that. He was wondering what Stephen would have said if he could have heard it.

"But it wasn't the money that was holding Whitney back at all," Miss Phoebe continued. "The truth is, I don't believe he ever thought about it. The real reason was that—that about a year ago, Whitney's wife died very mysteriously, and everybody thought for a while that he had killed her. It was foolish, of course; Whitney would never kill anybody. And Ronnie proved that he didn't in court with a judge and jury. You know about that, Mr. Carter?" she interrupted herself to ask.

Jefferson nodded. He was incapable of speech.

"Well," Miss Phoebe went on, "poor Whitney believed that, even though he had been proven innocent in court, people might still think he was guilty, because the real murderer had never been found; and so he felt that he didn't have the right to ask Ronnie to marry him so long as he had that—that bar sinister across his name. And then, right after he'd told Ronnie this, and they had planned how they would work together to find out the truth that would clear him, Ralph Marsden admitted to Ronnie that he had a letter from Ruth Hamilton —that was Whitney's wife—which would prove that she hadn't been murdered by anybody, but that her death had been a—a kind of accident. But he refused to give it to Ronnie unless she would promise to see to it that he got half of his grandmother's estate when she died."

She paused, as though expecting Jefferson to make some comment or ask a question at this point. When he did neither, she resumed:

"Poor Ronnie didn't know what to do. It wasn't that she cared about the money, but—there was something else." She lowered both her eyes and her voice with old-fashioned delicacy. "You see, Mr. Carter, there was something in that letter that—well, that proved that Ruth Hamilton hadn't been a very nice girl; and Ronnie didn't want Whitney to find that out, because she was afraid that the hurt of it would overbalance the satisfaction of proving his innocence in Ruth's death. So she asked me what I thought she ought to do."

"Just a minute, Miss Phoebe," the district attorney interrupted. "I already know about this letter from Ruth Hamilton to Ruth Marsden telling about her plan to poison her husband so that she and young Marsden could marry; it was found on Marsden's body last night

What I don't see is what it's got to do with your claim that you shot him."

"Why, don't you understand?" she asked in mild surprise. "I knew that while it might hurt Whitney at first to find out the truth, he'd get over it, because you can't live with the dead, and besides, Ronnie means more to him now than Ruth ever did; I'm positive of that. But I didn't want Ronnie to have to pay the price for that letter that Ralph was demanding; it wasn't fair. Besides, the money isn't to go to her; it's to go to Whitney, although neither of them know that. Then last night real late, when I couldn't sleep for thinking about it all, I happened to notice a light over in Ralph's den, and knew that he must still be up. So I dressed and went over to the Marsden house to try to persuade him to give me the letter. Only he wouldn't do it; and so I—I shot him."

Jefferson was holding his head by this time. When he could trust himself to speak he asked:

"But, Miss Phoebe, why should you have done this? I mean, why should you have committed murder, the most serious crime on the calendar, to insure the happiness of two persons neither of whom had any claim on you? People don't do such things for comparative strangers."

"But they're not comparative strangers!" she protested, looking at him earnestly. "I've known Ronnie ever since she was a tiny baby; and Whitney—" She lowered her eyes again, while a faint pink flush suffused her cheeks. "I suppose I'll have to tell you everything, Mr. Carter. When I was a young girl, I—I was married secretly. Whitney Hamilton is my son."

"*What!*"

She nodded, while the faint pink in her cheeks deepened to rose color.

"My sister, Maime, didn't approve of my marriage," she went on rather hurriedly. "And so, after my—my baby was born, she forced me to give him up, and to have my marriage annulled. That's why nobody ever knew about it."

It took Jefferson a full minute to come up for air. Then he asked:

"Miss Phoebe, how old is Whitney Hamilton?"

"He'll be thirty-five in January."

"And if it isn't too personal a question, how old are you?"

"Sixty-five—I mean sixty-six." The correction was made with reluctant honesty.

"Then at the time of your marriage, you must have been about twenty-nine or thirty. Surely you were old enough to have stood up against your sister."

"You don't know our Maime. She's strong-willed."

Jefferson, looking back over his past acquaintance with "our

Maime," thought that this might be putting it mildly. However, in this particular instance, he was still unconvinced.

"My dear lady," he said, "if you had a son to whom you were so devoted that you would commit murder for him, you would never have given him up when he was an infant. What you have just told me is all very interesting and—er—ingenious, but it simply doesn't carry conviction."

"You mean you don't believe me?" Miss Phoebe asked. Her lip was trembling, like a disappointed child's.

"I'm afraid I don't."

Miss Phoebe's expression took on a new determination.

"Then I'll prove it to you," she announced.

Curls bobbing, she bent over the knitting bag which she had been clutching so tightly, took something from it and laid it upon the district attorney's desk. It was an ancient revolver that looked as though it might have dated back nearly to the Civil War.

Jefferson stared at it incredulously.

"Where the hell—I beg your pardon—where did you get that thing?" he demanded.

"It was our pap's," Miss Phoebe explained with a touch of pride. "Maime always kept it loaded in case of burglars."

Jefferson picked it up and examined it.

"This revolver hasn't been fired," he said almost at once. "The muzzle and barrel are perfectly clean."

"I know," Miss Phoebe admitted. "I washed it with soap and water early this morning."

Jefferson laid the revolver down again.

"Miss Phoebe," he declared, "you're a most remarkable woman. Your loyalty to the people you are fond of is something that I find literally amazing; and I only hope that Whitney Hamilton is worthy of the sacrifice you stood ready to make for him. But before I could place you under arrest for the murder of Ralph Marsden, I would have to have more evidence of your guilt than your unsupported confession and"—he smiled slightly—"an antiquated revolver."

Miss Phoebe picked up the revolver and put it back into her knitting bag.

"You still don't believe me?" she asked, rising slowly.

"I still don't believe you," Jefferson affirmed. He rose also and, crossing the office ahead of her, opened the door for her. "But if it's any comfort to you," he added, patting her shoulder kindly as she was about to pass him, "I'll admit to you that we can't arrest your Whitney without further evidence; and if he's innocent, there will be no further evidence. Now go home, and stop reading such lurid fiction."

She smiled up at him.

"I *know* Whitney is innocent," she said confidently, and left.

Jefferson returned to his desk chair, sat down heavily and once more clutched his head in his hands.

"Women and the things they think of!" he muttered. "My God!"

But the next instant a look of amazed consternation overspread his face, and he sprang up again.

"Brooks!" he shouted. "Brooks!" And as his secretary appeared in the doorway leading to the outer office, "Catch that old lady who just went out of here and bring her back. Quick, before she gets into the elevator!"

The secretary hurried off, to return almost immediately with Miss Phoebe.

"What is it, Mr. Carter?" she asked. Her tone was half fearful, half expectant. "Have you decided to believe me after all?"

He waved her back to the chair from which she had risen less than a minute before.

"There's something I neglected to ask you, Miss Phoebe, he said without answering her question. "That revolver you just showed me: Where was it kept ordinarily?"

"In the drawer of the library table in the upstairs sitting room," she replied without hesitation. "Maime always kept it there in case of—"

"Yes, I know," he interrupted. "How many people, besides yourself and your sister, knew that it was kept there?"

"All our friends knew. Some of them used to tease us about it. Whitney said it was dangerous to keep it loaded," she added, speaking more to herself than to the district attorney. "I—I guess he was right."

Jefferson's eyes narrowed.

"So Hamilton knew about it too!" he exclaimed; then, before she could grasp the significance of this, he asked, "Think carefully, please, Miss Phoebe; did you notice whether this revolver was in its accustomed place last evening?"

"No, Mr. Carter, it wasn't."

"*It wasn't!* You're sure about that?"

She nodded.

"Of course I'm sure," she answered. "Didn't I just tell you I took it with me to try to frighten Ralph into giving me the letter? Only he didn't frighten the way I thought he would; and when he tried to take it away from me—the revolver, I mean—I—I must have pressed the trigger, and—"

Jefferson cut her short.

"Yes, yes, I know," he interrupted. "But never mind that, Miss Phoebe. I want you to leave this revolver here with me."

She opened the knitting bag obediently, took out the revolver and handed it to him.

"You're going to compare it with the bullet that killed Ralph to see if they match, aren't you?" she asked with the naivete of a child. "Well, they will match, Mr. Carter; you can depend upon that."

When she had gone, Jefferson summoned his secretary again.

"Take this gun down to the ballistics department, Brooks," he directed, "and ask Captain Martin to check it with the bullet Sergeant Forbes brought in about an hour ago."

Brooks took the revolver with amazement.

"Where did you get this baby cannon, Mr. Carter?" he inquired. "Not from that little old lady who was just in here?"

"Believe it or not, I did," Jefferson answered. "And without realizing what she was doing, she admitted to me that Whitney Hamilton knew about it, and had access to it."

The secretary whistled.

"Nice going, Mr. Carter!" he exclaimed admiringly. "If Captain Martin can show that the bullet fits it, you'll have all the evidence you need to arrest Hamilton."

Jefferson nodded, but he was surprisingly lacking in enthusiasm.

"And I'll feel like pretty much of a skunk," he added. "To borrow an expression of my brother Steve's, Brooks, I've just sold that little old lady down the river."

II.

"Ronnie, you promised you wouldn't do anything like that!" Whitney exclaimed. The girl had just told him of her agreement to pay her cousin twenty-five thousand dollars for Ruth Hamilton's letter.

"I know I did," she admitted. "But Ralph was threatening to burn the letter in front of my eyes. I had to do something—anything—to stop him. I was desperate."

"I'm not blaming you, dear." He smiled up at her face from his place on the porch steps at her feet. "He had you at a disadvantage." Then his expression sobered. "If I'd guessed he was going to browbeat you like that," he declared almost fiercely, "I'd have . . ." He let the sentence trail away unfinished.

"Whitney," Ronnie began uneasily, "the papers said this morning that Miss Maime saw a man leaving our house by the side door last night. You—you didn't—"

"Good Lord, Ronnie!" He stared at her in horror. "You don't think that I—"

"No, of course not," she reassured him quickly. "That wasn't what I meant. I merely thought that you might have come over and managed to get the letter. It isn't there this morning; I looked."

"You think—the police?" he suggested.

"I don't know," Ronnie answered. "But, Whitney, if they have got it, and they should question you about it, you've got to tell them that you agreed to let me buy it from Ralph. If you don't—"

"If I don't," he finished for her, "they'll probably think I killed him to get it. I'm not so sure but what they don't think that already."

"You mean—because of Mr. Carter's questions last night?"- she asked.

He nodded; then he inquired:

"Ronnie, who do you think did do it?"

"I don't know," she answered. "I've been thinking about that ever since it happened; and there just doesn't seem to be anyone who had sufficient motive. After all, while you may dislike and despise a person, you don't actually kill him for being—well, any of the things that Ralph was."

An antiquated electric coupe drew up to the curb, and Miss Phoebe got out. She was smiling as she advanced toward the two on the porch.

"Everything's all right now, children," she announced happily. "I was talking to the district attorney, Whitney, and he isn't planning to arrest you."

"Phoebe, how did you find out?" Whitney demanded in surprise. He had not been aware that she had even suspected he feared arrest.

"I asked him," Phoebe replied, although that wasn't strictly the truth. "That's one of the advantages of being an old woman," she added placidly. "You can ask people questions that they'd tell you otherwise were none of your business."

Ronnie began to laugh.

"Miss Phoebe, you're a darling!" she exclaimed; then she inquired, "You didn't by any chance ask him whom he does suspect?"

But before Miss Phoebe could reply, Miss Maime appeared in the doorway behind them.

"You just got back in time, Phoebe," she announced. "Dr. Richards wants to talk to you on the telephone."

12

DISCOVERY

(Thursday, 11:30 a.m. to 12:25 p.m.)

I.

Miss Phoebe sat down in the visitor's chair in Dr. Richards' consulting room and rested her knitting bag upon her knees.

"I came as fast as I could, Doctor," she said a little breathlessly. "It—it's nothing about our Maime you wanted to see me about, is it? She hasn't had anything the matter with her she's been keeping from me?" Dr. Richards was the Heisys' family physician as well as the Marsdens'.

"No, Miss Phoebe, it isn't because of Miss Maime that I asked you to come here," the doctor replied. "It's—another matter." He passed his hand over his bearded lips and chin. Now that he actually had the little old lady in his office, he wasn't sure exactly how to proceed.

Miss Phoebe noticed his hesitancy and, relieved that her sister was in no immediate danger, strove to help him.

"Do you mind if I knit while we talk?" she asked cozily, hoping that way to put him at his ease. She took from the knitting bag a half finished sock intended ultimately for some unknown member of her country's armed forces, and set to work.

The doctor watched the rhythmic flash of her bright steel knitting needles for several seconds; then he began abruptly:

"Miss Phoebe, the thing I want to talk to you about is—the murder of Ralph Marsden last night."

Miss Phoebe said nothing, but the knitting needles began to flash a little faster. The doctor noted this, and continued with more assurance:

"I have had the pleasure of your acquaintance for quite a few years now, dear lady, and during that time I have become convinced that you are a person of sympathy and understanding. More than that, you are a woman of generous impulses. You would not, for example, wish to see a man sent to prison—possibly to his death—for a crime of which he may be innocent."

Miss Phoebe nearly dropped a stitch. Was he about to drag Whitney back into the picture, just when the district attorney had assured her . . . ?

"Yes, Doctor," she murmured faintly. "I mean no, Doctor."

77

Dr. Richards smiled behind his hand. This was not going to be so difficult as he had thought at first.

"I was sure of it," he went on, unconsciously assuming the unctuous bedside manner upon which he prided himself. "And after all, the chance presence of a man near the scene of a—a murder is not a conclusive indication that he committed it."

This time Miss Phoebe did drop a stitch.

"But—but," she stammered, "it can't be proven that he was there."

"Precisely," he agreed. "And it won't be, Miss Phoebe, unless you, misled into a wrong idea of your civic duty, attempt to make a positive identification."

"I?" She stared at him uncomprehendingly.

He nodded.

"Have you seen this morning's papers?" he inquired.

She shook her head.

"Then let me read you the headlines." He reached for the newspaper that Helen Godwin had left upon the desk, and read aloud:

" 'Neighbor Sees Murderer Flee Scene of Crime. Elderly Spinster May Identify Murderer of Ralph Marsden.'

"Of course," he went on, laying the paper aside again, "it's quite possible that the newspapers have been exaggerating—they very often do in a thing like this—but in case the district attorney should attempt to trick or bully you into making positive identification of this man you saw leaving the Marsden house last night—"

Suddenly Miss Phoebe understood. He hadn't been referring to Whitney at all; he was referring to— She folded her knitting neatly, preparatory to putting it away.

"Doctor," she interrupted him, "there seems to be a misunderstanding. It wasn't I who saw you leaving the Marsden house last night. It was my sister, Maime."

"But—" He stared at her incredulously, his prominent eyes bulging. "Then—"

Abruptly he flung back his head and began to laugh uproariously...

II.

Stephen entered his brother's private office without the formality of either knocking or waiting to be announced, tossed his tropical straw hat with unfailing accuracy to the top peg of the clothes-tree in the corner and crossed to the district attorney's desk.

"Here are those startling new developments I promised you, Jeff," he announced, and spread three freshly developed photographic prints upon the top of the desk.

Jefferson glanced at them and snorted.

"A pun," he commented, "is absolutely the lowest form of wit.

What are these supposed to represent?"

"The first one's a fizzle," Stephen admitted, "but I've a notion the other two are pictures of the murderer of Ralph Marsden."

Jefferson looked more closely at the three prints. The first one was an indistinguishable blur, but the two others showed the somewhat vague but unmistakable outlines of the low foot of a bed, against which was standing a sheeted figure. The face, except for the eyes, was entirely hidden by the arrangement of the sheet; but one hand, where it held the edges of its shroud-like covering together, was clearly visible. The middle finger was decorated with a ring with a very large, dark stone.

"Where the devil did you get these?" the district attorney wanted to know.

Stephen explained. He also repeated what Mrs. Marsden had told him about her so-called hallucinations, and his own theory that some-one, who would profit thereby, had been attempting to prove her mental incompetence to administer the trust funds left in her care under her husband's will.

"So that's what you were driving at the other evening when you asked me who would profit if it was established that the old lady wasn't right in her head," Jefferson commented thoughtfully. He picked up the clearest of the three prints and examined it minutely.

"I told you at the time," he went on after a minute, "that the two people who stood directly to benefit by Mrs. Marsden's removal from the guardianship of the trust funds would be Ralph Marsden and Dr. Richards. That would imply—"

"—that since Ralph must have run into the ghost last night and been shot to prevent him from giving the show away," Stephen inter-rupted, impatient of his brother's slower thought processes, "it proves he couldn't have been playing ghost himself. And that leaves—Dr. Richards."

But Jefferson was not ready to agree to that.

"Not so fast," he admonished. "There are two possibilities on that score. The one is what you've just suggested. But the other is that Ralph might have been playing ghost, as you put it, and have been shot by someone else in the house who didn't recognize him.

"Now here's my theory," he went on, leaning back in his chair and clasping his hands behind his head. "We know from what Mrs. Marsden's nurse told us that Ronnie Marsden had promised to buy Ruth Hamilton's letter from Ralph. Well, suppose that afterwards she saw Hamilton and told him what she'd done, and he didn't like it. So he suggested instead that he come over that night and either look for the letter himself, or try to get it from Ralph by threatening him with that old revolver Miss Maime Heisy kept in her library table drawer. He knew Ralph was a coward, and would probably back down when threatened with physical violence."

"How do you know Miss Maime kept an old revolver in her library table drawer?" Stephen interrupted. "Or is that just another part of your theory?"

"I not only know that she kept one there, I've got it," Jefferson replied with satisfaction. He related the events of Miss Phoebe's surprising visit.

"But things didn't come off quite according to schedule," he went on without giving Stephen time to comment. "Hamilton arrived on the scene just as Ralph was finishing his ghost act, didn't recognize him and made a grab for him. Ralph, knowing what it would mean if his grandmother found out what he'd been up to, tried to get away; and in the tussle the gun went off and killed him."

"But," Stephen protested, "if any such rumpus went on, the whole house would have been roused, and the rest of them would know all about it."

"How can you be sure they don't?" Jefferson retorted. "Ronnie would lie in a minute to protect Hamilton; I haven't the slightest doubt of it. And you saw how quickly Mrs. Marsden flew to his defense when I tried to question him. As for the nurse, a few hundred dollars would buy her silence, while it would be entirely typical of her sort to double-cross them all on the sly with that letter business, to revenge herself on Hamilton for killing the man she wanted to marry. But if they'll all own up to the whole thing, I'm willing to make the charge only second degree murder, or even manslaughter, and let it go at that."

"Jeff, you sure are hell-bent on pinning this thing on Whitney Hamilton, aren't you?" Stephen observed. "But I can show you where you're wrong; at least, about Ralph's having been the ghost."

He moved around the desk and picked up the print that Jefferson had just laid down.

"You see that ring?" he asked, pointing to the hand of the figure in the picture. "Well, Doc Richards wears a ring like that. I saw it when I was talking to him yesterday morning." •

Jefferson frowned.

"That doesn't mean that Ralph didn't have a similar ring," he said after a moment. "And it doesn't put Maime Heisy's old revolver in Richards' possession. How do you explain that?"

"You're not sure yet that it was Miss Maime's gun that killed Ralph," Stephen reminded him. "Remember that."

Jefferson was about to reply when the telephone rang. He picked up the instrument, listened a moment to the voice at the other end, made a brief but satisfied reply, and replaced it upon its cradle.

"That was Captain Martin from the ballistics department," he announced. "He's just compared that revolver with the bullet that killed Ralph Marsden, and they check. So that ought to answer your objection about the gun."

"It doesn't prove that Whitney Hamilton used it," Stephen retorted stubbornly. "And if Richards happens to be the Heisys' doctor as well as the Marsdens', he'd have had plenty of chance to get it."

Jefferson threw up his hands in resignation.

"Steve, of all the mulish—" he began, and stopped. "Or wait a minute," he began again. "Maybe you're right at that about Richards having been at the Marsden house last night; and if he was, chances are he knows something he's afraid to tell because of this other business he's been up to.

"I think I'll go around to his office and see what I can get out of him," he went on. "In the meantime, you can go out to the Heisys' and find out whether or not he was their doctor, just to satisfy yourself."

Stephen crossed to the clothestree and retrieved his hat.

"I'll do more that that," he promised. "While I'm out there, I'll stop at the Marsdens' and find out whether or not Ralph had a ring like that, just to satisfy you."

III.

"Well, you see, Mr. Carter, it's this way," Miss Maime said in response to Stephen's question. "We buried our first doctor shortly after our pap died; and we buried our second doctor last December a year ago. So when Phoebe slipped on the ice and sprained her ankle the next February, we thought we'd call in Dr. Richards, because we knew the Marsdens had him and thought a lot of him. We've had him ever since."

"I sure hope you won't have to bury him," Stephen observed piously. Then he added, "I don't guess you have to send for him right often?"

"Not very often," Miss Maime concurred. "He looked after my rheumatism last winter, and he looked after Phoebe's hay fever last summer. He stopped in one day last week after he'd been to see Mary Marsden, to ask if Phoebe didn't soon want her injections for this summer; but I guess that was the first he'd been here since last March."

The first part of her last sentence had caught Stephen's attention.

"Miss Heisy," he asked, "did Dr. Richards know about the revolver you keep in case of burglars?"

"Oh, lands, yes!" she replied promptly. "He teases me about it still; says I wouldn't know how to shoot it if I did see a burglar. He's right about that, too," she added, "but the burglar wouldn't know it."

Stephen tried not to let his eagerness show in his next question.

"I don't guess you've seen Dr. Richards to talk to since Ralph Marsden was killed?" he suggested.

"No, we haven't," Miss Maime replied. She nearly always used the plural pronoun, Stephen noticed; but whether this was meant to refer to her sister and herself or was merely the editorial "we" he was unable to decide. "But that reminds me," she went on. "That Nurse came over here early this morning, pretending she wanted to call him up for Mary Marsden and that the Marsdens' telephone was out of order. But she didn't fool me any, not when I know they've got two telephones over there. And besides, Mary Marsden's phone's on the same line as ours; if hers had been out of order, ours would have, too. What that girl really wanted was to find out what she could about that man I saw last night. But she didn't get anything out of me."

She clamped her lips shut defiantly after the last word; then a startled expression crossed her face, as though she had suddenly realized that her last statement had carried with it the implication that there might have been something for the nurse to "get."

"If you'd like to see that revolver, Mr. Carter, I'll get it for you," she offered by way of changing the subject. "It's just upstairs in the sitting room."

But Stephen stopped her as she was about to rise.

"I don't guess it's there any more, Miss Heisy," he said. "I—I'm afraid my brother's got it."

"The district attorney!" Miss Maime's voice rose at least two octaves. "How did he get it?"

"Your sister, Miss Phoebe, brought it to his office this morning."

For one of the few times in her life Miss Maime was utterly speech-less. Her eyes and her mouth flew open together in blank incredulity.

"Is—is our Phoebe crazy?" she managed finally.

"No, ma'am, I don't think so," Stephen answered carefully. Then he asked, "Miss Heisy, in what room is your telephone located?"

"It's in the upstairs sitting room," she answered automatically.

"Thank you," he said, and left before she could recover sufficiently to ask why he had wanted to know.

IV.

Helen Godwin opened the front door of the Marsden house in response to Stephen's ring. She informed him that Mrs. Marsden was sleeping, but inquired whether he would care to speak to Miss Veronica instead. When he told her that he would, she conducted him into the library to wait. When Ronnie came into the room a minute or so later, her expression was grave, but not apprehensive. Apparently, Stephen thought, she was not uneasy at the prospect of being questioned by the brother of the district attorney. But her first words, when she spoke, indicated that she was not thinking of him in that capacity.

"I'm sorry Gram can't see you at present, Mr. Carter," she said. "The shock of Ralph's death was beginning to make itself felt, and so about an hour ago Miss Godwin gave her a sleeping tablet. I don't know whether I can substitute for her or not; I must admit I'm not very familiar with her private affairs."

"That's not what I came to see her about this time, Miss Ronnie," Stephen replied. "I wanted to ask her a question or two about your cousin."

"Oh!" The expression in the girl's eyes became suddenly guarded. "What is it you want to know?" she asked. "Perhaps I may be able to tell you."

"I was wondering," he answered, "whether he owned a large tiger's-eye ring, or a ring with any other kind of large, dark stone in it."

"No, I'm quite sure he didn't," Ronnie declared at once. "Ralph never cared for jewelry of any kind." Then she asked, "Why did you want to know that, Mr. Carter?"

"Because," he told her, "I've a right good reason for believing that the person who killed him was wearing a ring like that."

The look of relief in the girl's face was unmistakable; and Stephen knew without having to ask that neither did Whitney Hamilton possess such a ring. He decided upon a bold move.

"Miss Ronnie," he inquired, "what time was it when you talked with your cousin last night?"

"About half past—" she began, then checked herself. "What makes you think I talked with my cousin at all last night?" she demanded, on guard again.

"I'm sorry," he apologized, "but I'm not allowed to tell you that. But I know that you did talk to him, and what you talked about. You see," he added by way of convincing her of the truth of these statements, "we've got Mrs. Hamilton's letter."

"Oh!" Ronnie lay back in her chair and closed her eyes. For a moment she looked as though she were going to faint. Then she opened her eyes again and looked earnestly at Stephen.

"It was about half past eleven when I saw Ralph," she admitted. "Whitney—Mr. Hamilton and I had decided to offer him twenty-five thousand dollars for that letter. I went into Ralph's den last night to tell him so, and he agreed to accept. I was to have paid him the money this morning as soon as the banks opened. So you see," she finished, "everything was settled so far as Whitney and Ralph and I were concerned, and the letter could have had nothing to do with his death."

"Did you see Mr. Hamilton again last night after you'd talked to Ralph?"

"No," she answered. "That is, not until he heard the shot, and came over to find out what had happened."

"Then how did he know that everything was settled?"

Now that it was too late, Ronnie realized her slip.

"It's true that lawyers are the people who make the worst showing under cross-examination, isn't it?" she observed with a wan smile. "I see I may as well tell you the truth, Mr. Carter. Whitney didn't know I had offered to buy the letter from Ralph. In fact, he wouldn't even have known of its existence if he hadn't heard me talking about it to Miss Phoebe that morning. All he knew was that I was going to try to induce Ralph to give it to me. But you've got to believe me; he had nothing to do with Ralph's death. I'm positive of that."

"So am I, Miss Ronnie," Stephen told her, and felt amply rewarded by the look of gratitude she gave him. "You see, there was another person who talked to Ralph after you did; not the person who wore the ring I mentioned a while ago, but—"

He stopped as the telephone at Ronnie's elbow began to ring. She picked it up, but the next minute handed it to him.

"It's for you, Mr. Carter," she said. "I think it's your brother."

She watched him as he raised the receiver to his ear, heard his eager, "That you, Jeff? How'd you make out?" then saw his look of incredulous astonishment as the voice at the other end answered.

"Hold the line a minute," he directed. Then he turned to Ronnie, holding the instrument so that her voice would carry into the transmitter.

"Miss Ronnie," he asked, "have you seen Whitney Hamilton this morning?"

"Why, yes," she answered at once. "He's been with me practically ever since Ralph was killed. I only left him when Helen Godwin came out and told me you wanted—oh!" she broke off in sudden alarm. "He—he hasn't been—nothing's happened to him?"

"No, he's all right," Stephen assured her; then he added, "But the Heisys are about to bury their third doctor."

13

INQUIRY

(Thursday, 12:30 p.m. to 1:30 p.m.)

1.

Stephen opened the door to Dr. Richards' waiting room. He found Jefferson inside; also a number of plainclothesmen from detective headquarters. One of them was attempting to question the doctor's office nurse, a not unattractive little brunette, who was dabbing at her eyes with a handkerchief and sniffling.

"Where is he, Jeff, and how'd it happen?" Stephen asked, going over to his brother.

"He's in there." Jefferson jerked his head toward the closed door to the consulting room. "Stabbed through the throat. Doc Lufkin thinks the implement used may have been one of those sharp spike affairs used for filing receipts; although so far we haven't been able to find one on the premises. But of course the murderer could have taken it away with him. Probably did."

"Who found him?" Stephen inquired.

"The nurse, there, when she went to tell him I wanted to see him. It must have been a devil of a shock, even for a nurse."

"Can't she tell you who was with him last?"

"No. All she can say is that he was alive when she went out to lunch around eleven o'clock, and dead when she got back. She was just taking her hat and coat off when I came in and asked to see him."

"What time was that?"

"About half an hour ago, or about twenty minutes before I called you at the Marsden house. But Lufkin's placed the time of death between a quarter past eleven and a quarter to twelve, if that's what you're driving at. And I'll admit you did a smart piece of work in getting Ronnie Marsden to furnish Hamilton with an alibi without even realizing what she was doing," the district attorney nodded grudgingly. "But you took a damned big chance, in case she hadn't known where he was."

Stephen smiled confidently.

"When I'm right sure a man's innocent, I can afford to take chances like that," he replied. "I guess you'll have to admit now that it's not very likely Hamilton killed Ralph Marsden."

85

"If you're inferring that the two murders were committed by the same person," Jefferson retorted, "it doesn't look exactly as though your own favorite suspect could have killed him, either."

Stephen let that pass.

"Mind if I talk to the nurse?" he inquired.

"Help yourself; but if you can get anything more out of her than a bunch of sniffles, you're good."

Stephen crossed to where the girl was sitting, motioned aside the exasperated plainclothesman who was attempting to question her and took his place.

"I don't guess you feel right good in your mind after what you've been through, miss," he began in his most ingratiating drawl, "but if you'll try to put up with us a few minutes longer, I'll make them let you go home."

The nurse glanced up, intrigued by the rich Southern accent; then, perceiving that she had been addressed by an exceedingly personable young man instead of by a red-faced detective, she brightened considerably.

"But I don't know anything," she protested in a remarkably accurate imitation of Katherine Hepburn. "Really I don't."

"Of course you don't," Stephen agreed. "You were out to lunch when it happened. By the way, do you always go out to lunch at eleven o'clock?"

"No," the nurse answered, wondering hopefully whether he might be inquiring from any personal interest. "Usually I don't go out until half past twelve, after the doctor's been out for his. But today he told me I could go early."

Stephen changed the subject with abruptness.

"Did you generally answer the doctor's telephone?" he inquired. "Or did he answer it himself when he was in the office?"

"I answered it, always," she replied. "Dr. Richards didn't like to be disturbed when he was busy with a patient, and even when he wasn't— Well, you know how some people are; they'll call up a doctor and waste his time when there's nothing the matter with them at all."

"It must be downright annoying," Stephen said sympathetically. "Were there many calls this morning?"

"Only two; people who wanted the doctor to call this afternoon when he made his house visits. Shall I give you their names?"

"I don't guess that'll be necessary," he told her; then he asked, "What did the doctor do about the telephone when you were out to lunch?"

The girl smiled faintly.

"He usually let it ring," she answered. "Or else he'd just take the receiver off the hook."

Stephen smiled, too, but refrained from commenting upon this sidelight on the doctor's professional ethics.

"Did Dr. Richards see his patients by appointment?" he asked instead.

"In the mornings, from ten to a quarter of twelve, yes. When he came back from lunch, he stayed in the office about an hour to see any patients who might have come in without an appointment; then he'd go out to make his house visits from half past one till— Oh!" she interrupted herself, as though she had suddenly remembered something, and picked up a partially filled in chart from the desk in front of her. "You'll want to see this, of course! It's the list of this morning's appointments."

Stephen examined the chart and noted that the section from ten forty-five to one was vacant.

"Did the doctor ever see people in the mornings without an appointment?" he asked next.

"Sometimes," she admitted, "if he had a free space to work them in."

"Were there any like that today?"

The girl thought for a minute.

"There was Miss Godwin," she said then. "She's another nurse, who's on a case of Dr. Richards'. She came in about a quarter of eleven, just after the last scheduled patient left. When she found the doctor wasn't busy, she just walked in without waiting for me to announce her. But she didn't kill him," she added quickly, as though fearful lest that might be what he was thinking. "She only stayed about five minutes; and besides, he was alive after that, for he called me in almost as soon as she'd gone and told me I could have my lunch hour early."

"I see," Stephen said. "Well, thank you very much, miss. You've been a right big help. Jeff," he called to his brother, who had just returned from the inner office, where he had gone to consult with the coroner, "I'm letting this young lady go home. She's told me everything she knows."

The nurse put on her hat and coat and left the office with a feeling of disappointment. He hadn't even inquired whether she had a telephone.

"Steve," Jefferson asked admiringly, "how do you do it? And what in heaven's name did she tell you?"

Stephen smiled serenely.

"It's an art," he replied. "Remind me some time to give you a couple of lessons. As to what she told me—well, she told me that Richards knew his murderer was coming, and wanted to be alone with him."

"*What!*" The voice of the detective who had first attempted to question the nurse became falsetto. "She knew all that, and she was holdin' out on me?"

"She didn't realize she knew it," Stephen exclaimed. "What she actually said was that Richards sent her out to lunch early today— over a full hour early; which shows he was expecting somebody he wanted to be alone with. Then she showed me today's appointment schedule, and the time after a quarter to eleven was vacant, proving that the person he was expecting wasn't a regular patient. And since she admitted she always took all the incoming telephone calls, it proves that this person didn't call up this morning to make a last-minute appointment. So it looks like either Richards sent for him himself, or was told by Miss Helen Godwin that he was coming."

"Helen Godwin!" Jefferson fairly yelped. "That's the nurse out at the Marsden house! Where does she come into this?"

"According to the office nurse," Stephen replied, "it looks like she came in around a quarter of eleven this morning, stayed about five minutes and then left again."

Jefferson started toward the door.

"Come on," he commanded. "We're going out there and have a talk with her."

II.

This time it was Ronnie who opened the front door.

"Gram's awake now," she smiled as she saw Stephen. "If you want to talk to her . . . "

"I don't guess we'll need to bother her, Miss Ronnie," he said with an answering smile. "It's her nurse, Miss Godwin, we want to see this time."

"But first," Jefferson put in, "we'd like to ask you one or two questions if we may, Miss Marsden."

"Certainly," Ronnie said a little wonderingly, but Stephen noticed that the look of guarded watchfulness he had observed before did not spring into her eyes this time. She led the way into the library.

"Now what is it you want to know, Mr. Carter?" she inquired when they had seated themselves.

"It's just a detail or two about last night," Jefferson replied. "You told me when I questioned you at the time, Miss Marsden, that about a minute elapsed between the time when you heard the shot that killed your cousin Ralph and the time when you opened your bedroom door and looked out into the hall. Would that have been long enough, do you think, for anyone to have left the den and run down the hall to, let us say Miss Godwin's room next to your grandmother's?"

"Why, yes, I suppose so," Ronnie admitted. "But Helen was there, and would have seen them. It would have been easier for them to have gone into Ralph's bedroom, or down the back stairs."

Jefferson made no comment.

"You say your room is directly opposite the nurse's?" he asked instead.

"Not exactly," she corrected. "My room is opposite Gram's, while Helen's is across from Ralph's room; or more precisely, across from the bathroom between his room and mine. You see," she added by way of explanation, "the den and the back stairs are at the end of the house; then on one side of the hall, coming front, there's Ralph's bedroom, the bathroom, and my bedroom, with another bathroom and a guest room beyond that; while on the other side, there's the big linen closet, Helen's bedroom, Gram's bedroom and bath, and her sitting room."

"I see," the district attorney nodded; then he went on, "You say that Miss Godwin opened her bedroom door at about the same time you opened yours. Did you happen to notice what she was wearing at the time?"

"What was she wearing?" Ronnie repeated, as though she was wondering what possible significance might lie behind the question. "Why, I—I think she was wearing her uniform. Yes, I'm positive that she was."

"Wasn't that a little unusual for that time of the night?"

A look of sudden comprehension leaped into the girl's eyes.

"Mr. Carter!" she exclaimed. "You're not suggesting— But Helen wanted to marry Ralph!"

Stephen put in a word.

"You told me when I was here a while ago that it was around half past eleven last night when you spoke to Ralph and arranged to buy that letter from him," he said, using that means of passing the information along to Jefferson. "But Miss Godwin saw him after that, because she knew all about the arrangement when she talked to us. That means she must have talked to him between midnight and half past two; and that so far as is known, she was the last person to be with him before he was killed."

Jefferson looked decidedly interested at this; but when he spoke, it was to address Ronnie.

"Just one more question, Miss Marsden," he said, "then I think we'll have the nurse in here: My brother told you, I suppose, about Dr. Richards' death. Well, we've discovered that Miss Godwin was the yast person known to have been with him, too; that she called at his office at about a quarter to eleven. Do you happen to know what time she left the house here this morning, and what time she returned to it?"

"I'm afraid I don't," Ronnie admitted. "I was over at the Heisys' part of the morning, and Miss Maime asked me to stay there for lunch.

When I called up to tell Gram, Helen answered the phone and said that Gram had been feeling nervous, and she had just given her a sleeping tablet."

"At what time was this?"

"I really didn't notice the time, but the Heisys' generally have lunch at twelve o'clock."

"It must have been earlier than that today," Stephen put in, "because you were talking to me by a quarter past twelve."

"Yes, that's right," Ronnie agreed. "And now that I think of it," she added, "I believe they did have lunch earlier than usual, because Miss Phoebe wanted to go out somewhere, and Miss Maime insisted that she have something to eat before she went."

"Could it have been as early as eleven o'clock?" Jefferson inquired.

"I suppose it could have been," she admitted. "Or close to that."

"I see," the district attorney observed, as though satisfied. "And now suppose we have Miss Godwin in, and find out what she's got to say for herself."

"I'll call her," Ronnie offered, and left the room.

"You going to arrest her, Jeff?" Stephen inquired while they waited.

"I don't know yet," Jefferson replied. "If I do, I'll have to bluff it through, because I haven't even got a John Doe warrant with me."

"But you think she's guilty?"

The district attorney shrugged.

"She's almost got to be, now that Richards' death put both himself and Hamilton out of the running," he answered. "There doesn't seem to be anybody else left to suspect."

They waited in silence, then, for Ronnie's return. But when finally she did come back into the room about ten minutes later, she was alone.

"I've looked everywhere, and I can't find Helen anywhere in the house," she announced. "And Gram says she hasn't seen her since she woke up. I'm awfully afraid, Mr. Carter, that she's run away."

14

THEORY

(Friday, 11:15 a.m. to 12 n.)

I.

Jefferson tossed his hat in the general direction of his office clothestree; but, having been directed with less accurate aim than Stephen's, it fell short of its intended mark and landed on the floor.

"Damn inquests, anyway!" he grumbled. "Here we've wasted the better part of a morning on that one, and what have we got? 'Murder at the hands of some person unknown, but the jury respectfully suggests that the nurse, Helen Godwin, be found and held for questioning.'" He mimicked the voice of the pompous little foreman of the coroner's jury. "We got that much by ourselves. What we haven't got is Helen Godwin."

"Hasn't there been any trace of her yet?" Stephen asked.

"Not a single, solitary trace," Jefferson answered in disgust. "Forbes has inquired at both railroad stations and the three bus terminals, and she didn't leave from any of them, either with or without a ticket. Since she was wearing her nurse's uniform when she lit out and didn't take any other clothing with her, the station attendants would have spotted her. The same thing holds true for all the hotels in town, too."

"Maybe she stopped at her own apartment, or wherever it is she lives when she's not on a case, and changed her clothes," Stephen suggested.

"Forbes checked on that, too," Jefferson replied. "She's got a room at a private boarding house where the landlady seems to make it a matter of pride to know all her lodgers' comings and goings; and she swears that the Godwin girl hasn't been there for over a week. The only thing I can think of is that she might have thumbed a ride with some passing car; so I'm having a request made every hour over the radio that any car picking up a nurse in this city yesterday afternoon get in touch with the police here at once. But so far there hasn't been any response."

"You know, Jeff," Stephen said thoughtfully, draping a leg over the arm of the chair in which he was sitting, "somehow I've got an idea that she hasn't left town at all, but is lying low somewhere right near home."

"Quite possibly," Jefferson agreed. "But the question is, where?"

Stephen slumped deeper into his chair and lighted a cigarette.

"Let's see," he mused as he shook out the match. "If I was a nurse and was afraid of being arrested for murder, where would I go to hide?"

"All right; where would you? But don't tell me you'd hide in a hospital where one nurse more or less wouldn't be noticed; the things aren't run that way."

"No," Stephen said. "I think I'd go to somebody I had a claim on, and make them take me in."

"Forbes did go around to see all her known friends, and every blessed one of them's in the clear."

"What about her enemies I mean, somebody she might have something on?"

"Talk sense. Anybody like that would be only too glad for the chance to give her away, and would come straight down here."

"Not if she had enough on them, they wouldn't."

Before the district attorney could comment, his secretary looked into the room.

"Miss Heisy to see you again, Mr. Carter," he announced, grinning.

Jefferson groaned.

"If that woman's here to confess to the murder of Richards this time, I'll go crazy!" he declared.

"No, Mr. Carter, I'm not," Miss Phoebe told him, entering upon the secretary's heels. She thanked Stephen with a smile as he quickly disengaged himself from his own chair, and pushed forward another, more comfortable one for her. "I've come to tell you who the man was our Maime saw leaving the Marsden house the night Ralph was shot."

"You mean Miss Maime's remembered something about him that made her realize who he was?" Jefferson asked.

She shook her curls in denial.

"No," she answered, "but I found out. He was Dr. Richards."

Although this was not exactly news to either Jefferson or Stephen, they were both interested.

"How did you find out, Miss Phoebe?" Jefferson inquired.

"He told me so himself," she replied. "Although of course he didn't realize at the time that he was telling me. You see, he thought it was I who saw him leaving the house instead of Maime; and so he sent for me to try to get me to promise not to say anything further."

"Well, I'll be—" Jefferson began, and checked himself just in time. "When did all this happen?"

"Yesterday morning in his office at—let me see—it must have been around half past eleven o'clock."

"*What!*" The district attorney jumped as though something had stung him. "But—but that was right—just about the time when he was killed!"

"Yes," Miss Phoebe agreed placidly, "I know."

"How long were you there with him?"

"About five minutes; maybe ten."

"But that leaves only about five minutes—" Jefferson began, and stopped. "Tell me, Miss Phoebe," he said, "when you left the office, was there anyone in the waiting room?"

But again she shook her head.

"No," she answered, "the waiting room was empty."

Stephen and Jefferson looked at each other in blank bewilderment.

"Would it be presumptuous of me to offer a—a theory?" Miss Phoebe ventured timidly.

"Of course not," the district attorney assured her. "Go right ahead."

"Well, then," Miss Phoebe began, having evidently decided to put her suggestion in the form of a question, "couldn't it be that Dr. Richards killed Ralph Marsden? Somebody was trying to make Mary Marsden look as if she was losing her mind by pretending to be a— a ghost or something; and he, being her doctor, could very easily have been the one who was doing it, on account of that money old Mr. Marsden left him in his will. If Ralph saw him and recognized him the other night, he might have shot Ralph to keep him from telling.

"Then, when he thought I had seen him leaving the house, he sent for me and tried to make me promise not to say anything more, like I just told you; only he discovered after it was too late and he'd given himself away that it was Maime who had seen him. So couldn't he," she reverted to the question form again, "realizing that I knew all about him now and that I might tell you or somebody else, have decided that the—what s the expression they use?—that the game was up, and made up his mind to kill himself instead of waiting to be arrested?"

"I think not, Miss Phoebe," Jefferson told her. "You're right about Dr. Richards' having been the one who was trying to make it appear that Mrs. Marsden was suffering from hallucinations—Steve here has proved that. But we don't think he killed Ralph Marsden, and we know that he didn't kill himself. Someone was either hiding in the patients' waiting room when you went out yesterday, or else came in immediately after you left." He was careful not to mention Helen Godwin by name. So far he had let it be known only that she was wanted for questioning, and had said nothing about the possible murder charge.

"However," he continued, thinking that he perceived the real motive behind the old lady's visit, "if you're afraid that we may be suspecting Mr. Hamilton again, you can put your mind at rest. We know that he was having lunch with you, your sister and Miss Marsden at the time that Dr. Richards was killed; and since we also know now that it was Dr. Richards whom Miss Maime saw leaving the Marsden house that night, that lets Mr. Hamilton out on that score, too." He smiled at her reassuringly.

She smiled in return.

"Well, I'm glad you're convinced now that Whitney is innocent," she said, preparing to leave, "although of course I knew he was from the very beginning. But I'm sorry you don't like my theory," she added a little wistfully. "I was hoping it would—well, sort of settle everything without hurting anybody."

Jefferson's secretary put his head in at the door to the office.

"Excuse me, Mr. Carter," he began, "but I nearly forgot, and I thought I'd better tell you before it slipped my mind again: Old Mrs. Marsden called up while you were at the inquest, and said she wanted to see Mr. Stephen as soon as he could come out."

"Thanks, Brooks," Jefferson said; then to Stephen: "You'd better run out there right away, Steve, and see what she wants. It's just possible she may have had some word from the nurse."

"Can't I give you a lift, Mr. Stephen?" Miss Phoebe offered. "I've got my electric coupe outside, and we can conserve gasoline and rubber that way."

"Thank you, Miss Phoebe," he accepted. "That's right kind and patriotic of you."

He followed her down to the waiting coupe and got in beside her. But he rose at once with much greater alacrity than he had sat down.

"Oh, I'm so sorry!" Miss Phoebe exclaimed contritely. "I must have left my knitting bag on the seat." She picked it up and placed it on her lap. "Now," she said.

Stephen sat down again, this time with more comfort.

"You know," Miss Phoebe observed as they rode along at a sedate fifteen miles per hour, "I still wish there was some way I could convince your brother of that theory of mine. It would explain everything so nicely without anybody's having to go to jail."

Stephen smiled.

"I wish you could, too, Miss Phoebe," he replied. "But I'm afraid it can't be that way."

"But the waiting room was empty when I came out," she persisted. "And if Dr. Richards was dead by a quarter to twelve, like the papers said this morning, there wouldn't have been time for anyone else to have come in after I left."

"There was at least five minutes," he pointed out. "Maybe longer. After all, the coroner can't place the time of death to the very minute. But there's another reason why we know that Dr. Richards' death couldn't have been suicide."

"Another reason?" She took her attention away from her driving long enough to glance at him questioningly.

"You see," he explained, "if it had been suicide, we'd have found the weapon somewhere near him. But there was no weapon of that sort anywhere in the room."

"Oh!" Miss Phoebe looked crestfallen. "I never thought of that!"

II.

"Well, Stephen," Mrs. Marsden said, "you did a nice job of clearing up that hallucination business. Now what have you got to report on the death of my grandson?"

Stephen hesitated. He wasn't sure just how much Jefferson would want him to tell.

"Not much just yet, I'm afraid," he answered conservatively. "You see, we're working by a process of elimination. So far we've eleminated Whitney Hamilton, and now Dr. Richards' death eliminates him—"

"Are you sure of that?" she interrupted him. "I rather thought, after you telephoned me yesterday morning about how those pictures turned out, that he might have killed Ralph."

"Then how's it happen *he* was killed?" Stephen countered. "It's not right likely we'd have two murderers in such a small group of people."

"Why not?" she demanded. "It seems to me that it's no more unlikely that there could have been no connection between Richards' death and Ralph's than that there could have been no connection between Ralph's death and Richards' attempting to scare me out of my mind by playing ghost."

There was logic in that, he had to admit.

"Sometimes," he said slowly, "I wonder if there isn't some sort of connection between all three of them."

"How do you mean?"

"Well," he tried to explain the thing that he sensed only vaguely himself, "suppose that while Dr. Richards was here that night, he saw and recognized the person who killed Ralph. Either that person knew that he'd seen him or her, or Richards had the bad sense to let him know it; and so they killed him to hush his mouth."

"That's possible," she admitted. "But then what was this person's motive for killing Ralph in the first place?"

"That," Stephen admitted unguardedly, "is the one weak link in our case."

"Oh!" she caught him up. "So you *have* got a case against somebody!"

"We're looking in every possible direction," he hedged.

"I see." She smiled grimly. "Big Brother's told you to keep your mouth shut."

"Yes, ma'am," Stephen admitted meekly.

She glanced out of the window for a minute. Suddenly she asked: "Stephen, why are the police looking for Helen Godwin?"

"Jeff wants to ask her some questions."

"Does he think she killed Ralph?"

"I kind of guess he does."

"What do you think?"

"I guess I think so, too."

The old lady snorted.

"Nonsense!" she exclaimed. "Why, the girl wanted to marry Ralph. Why should she have killed him?"

"Like I said just now, that's our weak link. But maybe he decided all of a sudden that he didn't want to marry *her.*"

Mrs. Marsden shook her head.

"No," she said. "I dislike having to admit this about my own grandson, particularly now that he's dead, but Ralph was woman-crazy. He'd take anything with a skirt on that would have him. Besides, Helen Godwin was just his type: a little flashy, and full of—what is that expression you young people use? Just two letters, I believe it is."

"S.A." Stephen supplied, and wondered whether or not it would be necessary to explain what it meant.

Mrs. Marsden sniffed.

"I don't like it," she stated flatly. "It sounds too much like those other two letters they use to advertise a certain brand of bath soap. But anyway, Helen had it; and Ralph would have married her in a minute if he'd thought he could have gotten my consent."

"And could he have?" Stephen inquired.

"I don't know," she answered honestly. "Helen was far from the type of girl I'd have picked out for him; but sometimes I think it would have been better to have had him safely married to her than to risk a repetition of—the Ruth Hamilton sort of thing."

She glanced out of the window again, but this time only for a second or so.

"And now I suppose you're wondering," she went on almost at once, "why I should have kept her around when I didn't approve of her. Well, I'll tell you why: I wanted to have both her and Ralph where I could keep an eye on them. If I'd sent her away, there was no telling what might have developed. And besides," she added, either from a sense of practicality or a desire to soften the effect of her preceding sentence, "she was a good nurse."

"Mrs. Marsden," Stephen asked, "do you think Miss Godwin was actually in love with your grandson?"

"I don't know," she replied reflectively. "She was at least fond of him; I feel sure of that. Why?"

"I was just wondering," he explained, "whether Dr. Richards could have shot Ralph, and Miss Godwin, knowing that he had done it, could have killed him. But no," he contradicted himself; "I don't guess that's any good, either. If it was, she wouldn't have taken the gun back to the Heisys' for him the next morning."

"She—*what?*" Mrs. Marsden was staring at him incredulously.

Stephen explained about the revolver. In doing so, he had also to explain about Miss Phoebe's attempted confession to the murder of Ralph in order to save Whitney Hamilton.

"Phoebe Heisy's an old fool!" Mrs. Marsden declared when she had heard. "Or maybe she isn't, at that," she amended almost in the next breath. "I think enough of Whitney myself to want to see my own granddaughter married to him; and I believe that Phoebe, even if she is an old maid, looks upon him as she would upon her own son. Maybe in her place . . ."

She didn't finish the sentence, but for the third time turned and stared out of the window. She remained that way so long that Stephen began to wonder whether she had forgotten his presence.

"But you see, Mrs. Marsden," he ventured by way of drawing her thoughts and attention back to her surroundings, "since we know definitely that it was Miss Maime Heisy's gun that was used, and since Miss Godwin made an excuse to go over there the next morning to the room where it was ordinarily kept—"

"Stephen," she interrupted him, "you're my lawyer, and it's up to you to tell me what I want to know whether Jeff likes it or not. Just how much of a case have you got against Helen Godwin?"

"We can prove by her own admission that she was the last person known to have seen Ralph alive," he replied. "We can show that she had an opportunity to return the gun the next morning. And we can prove that she visited Dr. Richards at his office around a quarter to eleven yesterday morning; and we can show that, after coming back here and administering a sleeping tablet to you, she had ample opportunity to go back there while you were sleeping and Miss Ronnie was next door having lunch at the Heisys'. And in addition to that, her disappearance is a right strong argument in favor of her guilt."

"In other words, all circumstantial evidence."

"Yes, ma'am; but we're not through yet. And if Miss Godwin was helping Dr. Richards to frighten you, as I'm sure she was—"

But she interrupted him a second time.

"Helen Godwin didn't take any gun over to the Heisys' yesterday morning," she declared. "I saw her go, and her hands were both empty. She merely went over there to find out if she could whether the man Maime Heisy had seen was Dr. Richards. And she didn't kill him, either. She was right here giving me a sleeping tablet at a quarter past eleven. I remember noticing the time."

"She could have gone after you were asleep. Dr. Richards wasn't killed until after half past eleven."

"I thought the papers said it was between a quarter after eleven and a quarter to twelve."

"Yes, ma'am, they did. But Miss Phoebe Heisy told us this morning that she was with him from half past eleven until about twenty of twelve; and he was alive then. So if Miss Godwin left here around twenty past eleven, she'd have had plenty of time to reach the office by twenty to twelve."

This time, instead of looking out of the window, Mrs. Marsden lowered her eyes to her hands where they were clasped about the gold knob of her cane.

"Ralph used to be genuinely fond of her," she muttered, evidently communing with herself. "And he wasn't all bad. I don't think he'd have wanted—"

She broke off, and turned back to Stephen.

"Helen Godwin is innocent," she stated, "and I can prove it. You can tell that brother of yours that if he attempts to charge her with murder, I'll go into the witness box and say that she was with me at the time Richards was killed. I'm not so infirm that I can't go out when I have to."

"But you were asleep at the time," Stephen protested.

"I'll swear that the sleeping tablet didn't take effect until after half past eleven. Listen, Stephen." She leaned forward in her chair, her hands gripping the knob of the cane until her knuckles showed white. "I'm not going to see that girl tortured by a court trial—maybe worse. You've got to convince Jeff that Dr. Richards killed Ralph, and then committed suicide afterwards."

"It's right odd, now," Stephen observed; "that was the very same idea Miss Phoebe had when she came into the office. But we couldn't accept it, because the weapon that was used to kill Richards had been taken away by the murderer."

"Then you'll have to find some other way to make Jeff drop the case," she said determinedly. "I've just decided that I don't want my grandson's murderer found."

15

REALIZATION

(Friday, 2 p.m. to 2:15 p.m.)

I.

Detective Sergeant Forbes lowered his big frame into the chair facing the district attorney.

"It's still no go, Mr. Carter," he announced. He both looked and sounded completely discouraged. "That nurse has disappeared as completely as if—as if somebody had waved a magic wand over her and made her invisible."

Jefferson smiled briefly at this unexpected flight of fancy on the part of the usual phlegmatic sergeant.

"Somebody's hiding her somewhere," he said. "She couldn't have vanished like that on a minute's notice, and stay vanished, without help.

"By the way," he went on, "Steve suggested a while ago that instead of looking for her among her friends, we try her enemies. He got the idea that she may be forcing somebody she's got something on to give her protection. Think there's anything to it?"

"Sounds possible," the sergeant admitted. "The only trouble is, we'd probably have as hard a time finding that person as we're havin' finding her.

"And here's another thing, Mr. Carter," he continued, crossing one large leg over the other. "Even if we do find her, have we got enough evidence to charge her with either murder, and make the charge stick? So far as I can see, we can't prove a motive."

"I'll admit that's been the weak link in our chain so far," Jefferson acknowledged, "but I believe we can fix it up now. A while ago Miss Phoebe Heisy—that's the little one—came in here and told me that she'd been in Richards' Office as late as half past eleven yesterday morning; that he'd sent for her in the belief that she was the one who had seen him leaving the Marsden house the night Ralph was killed.

"Now here's my idea: You know we found a newspaper on his desk with both his and Helen Godwin's fingerprints on it. I believe that he and the Godwin girl together were working that scheme to make old Mrs. Marsden appear mentally deranged; and that when

99

she saw that story in the morning papers about Maime Heisy's having seen a man leave the house, she took it around to show him and to find out whether he'd been there doing his apparition routine.

"He must have convinced her, temporarily at least, that he hadn't been anywhere near the place, for she went away. But after she'd gone back to the Marsden house she got to thinking things over, and she wasn't so sure that he'd told her the truth. So she gave old Mrs. Marsden a sleeping pill so that she could sneak out again without being missed—she knew that Ronnie was next door having lunch with the Heisys, and would probably remain there for some time—and skipped back to Richards' office.

"She got there just as he was having his interview with Miss Phoebe, and heard him admit to her that he was the man Miss Maime had seen. So she hid somewhere, either in the building or just outside, until she saw Miss Phoebe leave. Then she went in and finished him."

"Because she thought he'd killed young Marsden?" Forbes asked.

"No; because she was afraid he'd seen her do it."

"But, Mr. Carter," the sergeant protested, "that brings us right up against motive again. Why should she have killed Marsden? She wanted to marry the guy."

"Yes," Jefferson admitted, "but suppose Marsden didn't share her ambition? Suppose he'd been willing to marry her in the first place only as a means of getting hold of his grandfather's money—you know he couldn't come into that until he was married. Well, when Ronnie Marsden offered to buy that letter of Ruth Hamilton's from him, he saw his way to come into a good-sized chunk of money without marrying anybody. So when the girl friend showed up a little later to see how he'd made out with Ronnie, he told her that the deal was off so far as she was concerned; and— Well, you know that type of woman, Forbes," he concluded; "she'll kill a man before she'll let him walk out on her."

The detective caressed his underlip reflectively.

"That's nice reasoning, Mr. Carter," he admitted after a minute. "The thing is, are you goin' to be able to prove it?"

"I'll prove it, all right, once I lay my hands on the Godwin girl," he said with confidence. "But as Steve would say," he grinned ruefully, "first catch your 'coon before you try to skin him."

The door from the outer office opened, and Detective Donovan walked in.

"They told me downstairs I don't have to keep an eye on the Heisy dame any more, Mr. Carter," he began. "It that right?"

"That's right," Jefferson affirmed. "The man she saw is dead now; it's not likely she'll be in any more danger."

"Okay." The detective turned to leave, then stopped.

"You know, Mr. Carter," he began again, "there's something screwy goin' on out at that place."

"You mean the Marsden house?" Jefferson asked.

"No, the one next door, where the old maid I was watchin' lives."

"What sort of thing?"

"Well"—the detective went over to a chair and sat down—"ever since yesterday afternoon the curtains in one o' the upstairs rooms have been pulled down like they were expectin' a blackout."

"What's so extraordinary about that?"

"Nothin', I guess, except that those curtains were up yesterday morning. And last evening, I noticed a hand puttin' one o' them up a couple of inches while it raised the window to let in a little air; and it didn't belong to either of the old maids."

"How do you know it didn't?"

"Because," Donovan explained, "I'd noticed that both o' them were wearin' dark clothes—the tall, skinny one black, an' the little one a sort o' purplish color. But this hand had a white sleeve about it, an'— Say!" he broke off, "what are you fellas starin' at me so for?"

They stopped staring at him and stared at each other.

"My God!" the sergeant exclaimed. "The nurse!"

Jefferson nodded.

"Steve was right," he said. "She must be forcing them to hide her, threatening to swear that the man Maime saw was Hamilton if they don't."

II.

Stephen slouched in his swivel chair and stared moodily at his feet propped upon the edge of the big roll-top desk in front of him. He was well aware that at that hour of the afternoon, instead of being home, he should have been at his law office attending to any stray clients who might happen along; but the puzzle of old Mrs. Marsden's inexplicable behavior still intrigued him.

Why had the old lady sent for him to inquire what progress was being made toward the discovery of her grandson's murderer, then barely fifteen minutes later told him that she didn't want the murderer found? Was she so convinced of Helen Godwin's innocence that she preferred to have the mystery of Ralph's death go unsolved, rather than that the girl should be charged with the crime? And if that was the case, was it possible that Helen might be innocent after all?

He removed his feet from the desk and, drawing a sheet of paper toward him, began to make out a time schedule of the nurse's activities for the morning of the doctor's death. If it could be shown that she had not committed that murder, it would follow that it was unlikely she had committed the other, either.

At a quarter to eleven she had gone to Richards' office, remained with him for about five or ten minutes, and gone away again.

At a quarter past eleven she had given Mrs. Marsden her sleeping medicine. The old lady's statement to that effect tallied with what Ronnie had told him when he had called at the house about an hour later.

Dr. Richards had not been killed until a quarter to twelve, or possibly a few minutes after; so much was attested to by Miss Phoebe's statement that she had been with him in his office from half past eleven to approximately twenty minutes to twelve. That would have given Helen half an hour to have left the Marsden house, returned to the doctor's office, and—

Or would it? If Helen Godwin had killed the doctor because she believed he had seen her shoot Ralph Marsden, then she must have overheard him admit to Miss Phoebe that he had been the man Miss Maime had seen fleeing from the Marsden house after the shooting; and to do that, she would have had to be at the office by half past eleven, or a few minutes after. That would have cut her time from half an hour to fifteen minutes, even granting that she had risked leaving before her patient had fallen asleep. And besides, what reason could she have had for going back to the office in the first place?

Then she had been back at the Marsden house by a quarter past twelve; it had been she who had answered the door when he had come to inquire about Ralph's possible possession of a ring like the one shown in the picture. Could she have killed Dr. Richards, disposed of the weapon, returned to the house and put on a clean uniform—there must almost certainly have been some blood on the one she had been wearing—within a space of less than twenty minutes? He could not allow her the full half hour between a quarter to twelve and a quarter after, since she had already returned to the Marsdens' before he had arrived. The more he thought about it, the more improbable it seemed.

But was Mrs. Marsden's conviction of the nurse's innocence sufficient reason for her to be willing to let the whole case go unsolved? Why had she not merely asked Stephen to prove the girl's innocence, instead of insisting that the entire investigation be dropped? Was there not, perhaps, some additional reason for this that the old lady had not seen fit to mention? But what possible reason could there be?

Juniper, the old colored servant who had accompanied Stephen when he had come North to take over Jefferson's private law practice, came into the room bearing a frost-covered glass upon a tray.

"Dis hyar heat's enough ter git a man down, Mistuh Stephen," he announced, "so Ah thought you might like a nice, cool julep."

Stephen looked up appreciatively.

"Juniper, you're either a mind-reader or a genius!" he exclaimed. "That's exactly what I need."

He took the tall glass from the tray, swirled its contents delicately and inhaled its fragrant mint bouquet before drinking. Juniper lingered in hope of conversation.

"Looks lak it might be fixin' ter rain befo' long," he observed experimentally. "Dey looks lak black clouds comin' up out yonduh."

"I hope so," Stephen said absently between sips. Then he asked, "Juniper, if some member of your family had been murdered, and you decided you didn't want the murderer found, what reason would you have?"

The colored man grinned toothily. He enjoyed being consulted on what he called "murder business."

"Well, now," he began carefully, "eff'n Ah knowed who done it, an' was right fond o' the pusson what had, or eff'n Ah knowed dat havin' 'em arrested would hurt somebody else Ah was right fond of—"

"What's that?" Stephen had swung around in his chair. "Say that again, Juniper!"

"Ah said," Juniper obliged, "dat eff'n Ah knowed who done it, an' was right fond—"

"Never mind," Stephen cut him short. "Juniper, you *are* a genius! You've just solved the Marsden-Richards murder case!"

16

DECISION

I.

Jefferson turned to Detective Sergeant Forbes.

"Run down the hall and swear out a bench warrant for the arrest of Helen Godwin," he directed. "We're going out there and pick her up right away before she slips through our fingers again."

The detective heaved his big frame out of the chair.

"What's the charge to be, Mr. Carter?" he inquired. "Murder, or just withholdin' evidence?"

The district attorney hesitated for a minute.

"Make it murder," he decided finally. "We might as well go the whole way at once, for I think we can make it stick."

"Can I go along, too, Mr. Carter?" Detective Donovan asked eagerly as the sergeant left the office.

Jefferson nodded.

"You certainly may, Donovan," he answered. "You've earned the right. And if you want to, you may serve the warrant." He did not add that personally he was not over-fond of arresting women, even when he was convinced that they were twice guilty of murder.

The door opened, and Stephen came into the office. Jefferson turned to him.

"You're just in time, Steve," he said. "Donovan's located the Godwin girl for us. And you were right about her forcing somebody to protect her. She's been hiding out at the Heisys'; probably threatening to drag Hamilton back into the case if they gave her away. We're going out there to pick her up as soon as Forbes gets back with the warrant."

But Stephen showed neither satisfaction nor enthusiasm.

"Jeff, you can't do it," he declared flatly.

"Why not?" Jefferson wanted to know. "You agreed with me that she was guilty, didn't you? In fact, you were the first one to turn up evidence against her."

"I know," Stephen admitted. "But I've changed my mind."

"Oh, you have!" the district attorney exclaimed with biting sarcasm. Then he changed his tone.

"Now look here, Steve," he began more patiently, "when you started out in this case by championing Whitney Hamilton, I let you get away with it because I felt sorry for the poor devil on account of his having been accused unjustly of murder once before; and I was only too glad to have him cleared this time. But that doesn't mean that you can try it on every suspect I pick out; I won't stand for it."

"You sound," Stephen observed, "as if you didn't care whether your suspect was guilty or not, just so you got somebody to stand trial."

"You know that isn't true!" the district attorney exclaimed with indignation.

"No," Stephen admitted honestly, "I don't guess it is. But Helen Godwin couldn't have killed Richards, Jeff. Here's how I know." He outlined his schedule of the nurse's movements between the hours of ten forty-five and twelve-fifteen of the preceding day. "So you see," he concluded, "there simply wasn't enough time for her to have gone back to Richards' office in time to overhear his conversation with Miss Phoebe at half past eleven on the one hand, or for her to have killed him around a quarter to twelve and gotten back to the Marsden house before I showed up there at a quarter past twelve on the other."

But Jefferson shook his head.

"That's all very good theoretically, Steve," he said. "But you've no right to whittle your time down so closely, nor to state it so arbitrarily. For example, how do you know it was exactly a quarter after twelve when you went over to the Marsdens'? Did you look at your watch?"

"Well, no," Stephen admitted. "But it was exactly twelve o'clock when I reached the Heisys'; I heard the noon whistles blow. And I stayed there about fifteen minutes—"

"But you can't be absolutely certain of that," Jefferson interrupted him. "If I know Maime Heisy, she'd have talked at least fifteen minutes straight before you got a chance to put a word in edgeways. More likely it was nearer half past twelve when you left there.

"And the same thing holds true of all the other times you've mentioned," he went on. "How do you know it was exactly a quarter past eleven when Helen Godwin gave Mrs. Marsden her sleeping medicine? Ronnie Marsden admitted that when the nurse mentioned it to her on the phone when she called up to tell her grandmother she was having lunch with the Heisys, it could have been as early as eleven."

"But Mrs. Marsden looked at her clock, and she says it was a quarter past when she took the medicine," Stephen told him.

But Jefferson waved that aside.

"Old ladies can't be depended upon for absolute accuracy in such things," he stated. "I've noticed that that clock in her room has a convex glass; if she was looking at it from an angle, the hands would appear to be pointing to a quarter past eleven, when in reality they were pointing to only ten or even five after. Then there was the time that Miss Phoebe arrived at the doctor's office. Can she swear positively that it was exactly eleven-thirty, and not eleven twenty-five or eleven-twenty?"

"That part about the clock is a knife that cuts both ways," Stephen pointed out. "If Mrs. Marsden was looking at it from the opposite angle, she might hae thought it said a quarter after when it really said twenty after. But it only makes five or ten minutes' difference either way."

"Not on your final time of twelve-fifteen, it doesn't," Jefferson retorted. "That's the one that matters most; and according to your own admission just now, it's the one you're least able to prove."

"I still think there wasn't time enough," Stephen insisted stubbornly. "Jeff, you've got to believe me: Helen Godwin didn't kill either Ralph Marsden or the doctor; I know she didn't."

His brother eyed him keenly.

"How do you know?" he demanded.

"I've just told you."

"No, you haven't. Steve, you're holding something back."

Stephen didn't answer.

Sergeant Forbes came back just then with the warrant.

"All set, Mr. Carter," he announced; then, as he saw Stephen, "Oh, hello, Mr. Stephen. Goin' along to see us make the pinch?"

"No, he isn't," Jefferson answered for him. "He's got some new idea into that fool head of his that the Godwin girl isn't guilty after all, and he's been trying to talk me out of arresting her."

Sergeant Forbes looked interested, and also a trifle doubtful.

"You've got some new evidence, Mr. Stephen?" he asked.

"No, Forbes," Stephen answered. "I haven't got a single bit of evidence."

"Then you suspect something," Jefferson guessed shrewdly. "Out with it; what is it?"

Again Stephen didn't answer.

Jefferson studied him for a long minute, then decided to change his tactics.

"You probably don't, at that," he pronounced. "You're feeling sorry for her because she's a woman, and because young Marsden and Richards were such a rotten pair to begin with; so you're trying to work a bluff."

"I am not!" Stephen denied indignantly. "I merely said I haven't got any actual evidence, and I haven't. But that doesn't mean I don't know—"

He caught himself just in time. Jefferson pretended not to have noticed.

"Come on, Forbes, Donovan," he said, winking at the two detectives over Stephen's head. "We may as well get out there before the rain starts."

"Jeff, you can't!" Steve protested desperately.

Jefferson turned in the doorway.

"I'll tell you what I'll do, Steve," he offered. "I'll go out there and mark time questioning the girl for half an hour. If at the end of that time you haven't called me to tell me what it is you've got on your mind, I'm placing her under arrest."

II.

"But, Phoebe," Miss Maime said, "'there's no reason why we've got to keep her here any longer. She can't make the district attorney believe it was Whitney I saw that night, now that you've shown him it was Richards."

"I know," Miss Phoebe admitted. "But we can't just turn her out, Maime. What would become of her?"

"That's no concern of ours," Miss Maime averred.

"But suppose she was arrested. You know the police are looking for her. That's why she's hiding."

"I hadn't thought of that," Miss Maime admitted. She got down on her knees and dived under the radio cabinet.

"What are you doing?" Miss Phoebe asked, watching her idly.

"I'm disconnecting this blamed thing. There's a thunderstorm coming."

"Oh, dear!" Miss Phoebe exclaimed. "I hadn't noticed. And my car's out there at the curb!" she added in dismay.

"You'll have to leave it there now," Miss Maime told her. "Likely you'd get it halfway to the garage when the Good Lord would strike it with lightning on account of the lies you've told the last few days."

"I haven't told any lies," Miss Phoebe declared stoutly. "Or at least," she amended, remembering certain statements she had made to the district attorney, "only one or two little white ones that didn't matter. I just haven't told everything I know; that's all."

"And you're not going to, either," Miss Maime pronounced, backing out from under the radio cabinet.

"Maime," Miss Phoebe asked without looking at her sister, "do you know how—how Ralph Marsden was killed?"

Miss Maime didn't answer.

"Do you, Maime?" Miss Phoebe persisted.

"Yes, I do," Miss Maime said shortly. "But I can keep my mouth shut, too, although there's them that think I can't."

It was the first and only mention the sisters ever made between them of that phase of the mystery.

"Where's Whitney?" Miss Phoebe asked presently. "Over at the Marsdens'?"

Miss Maime nodded.

"Why bother to ask?" she retorted.

There came a sudden unexpected ringing of the doorbell.

"Now who can that be?" Miss Maime exclaimed. "I didn't see anybody come up the walk. Phoebe, run upstairs and look out the sitting room window."

Miss Phoebe went. She hoped that, whoever it was, he wouldn't stay long. Otherwise she didn't see how she and Miss Maime were going to manage to sit with their feet up on chairs, the way they always did during a thunderstorm.

She came running down again just as a second peal sounded at the bell. She was fairly quivering with excitement.

"Maime!" she gasped. "It's the district attorney, and he's got two detectives with him!"

III.

Stephen sat alone in his brother's office. He was in a quandary. Fifteen of the thirty minutes that Jefferson had promised him were already gone, and he was no nearer to making up his mind than he had been at the beginning.

It was true, as he had told Jefferson, that he had no actual evidence to prove who had killed Ralph Marsden and Dr. Richards, but he was reasonably certain where he could get some. He thought back upon that blinding flash of realization that had come to him with old Juniper's words, and he marveled that he had not seen the truth long ago; that Jefferson had not seen it.

It had all been there staring them in the face from the very beginning. It had been in Miss Maime Heisy's story of the man she had seen—in what she had left unsaid rather than what she had said. It had been in Ronnie's account of how Whitney had overheard her telling Miss Phoebe of Ralph's attempt to bargain with her over Ruth Hamilton's letter, and again in Miss Maime's story of Helen Godwin's feeble excuse to use the Heisys' telepnone the next morning. Why, one clue to the whole thing had been in his hands even before it happened, when Mrs. Marsden had failed to call him until ten minutes after she had seen the white figure standing at the foot of her bed!

And the motive? That had been innocently betrayed by Miss Phoebe, when she had come to Jefferson's office the next morning and attempted to confess to the murder in a transparent effort to shield the man whom she looked upon as the son she had never had. Poor Miss Phoebe!

Stephen wished devoutly that he had never come to see the truth; it forced upon him a decision which he felt incapable of making. If he told what he knew, at least two people besides the actual murderer would suffer acutely; probably more than two. On the other hand, if he remained silent an innocent woman would be brought to trial and possibly convicted.

He had to admit that Jefferson's point about the time element, in the only argument he could advance on behalf of the nurse's innocence, had been a good one; for while he was satisfied that the schedule he had worked out was essentially correct, he knew that he would be unable to prove it so. Of course old Mrs. Marsden would stand by her statement that it had been a quarter past eleven when Helen had given her the sleeping tablet, but her very insistence might tell against her as a creditable witness. Besides, as Jefferson had pointed out, it was the last part of the schedule that mattered most; and Stephen knew that he himself could not actually swear that it had been as early as a quarter past twelve when the nurse had admitted him to the Marsden house.

Of course, if he were to undertake Helen Godwin's defense personally, he might be able to create a reasonable doubt in the minds of the jurors that would result in a verdict of not guilty. Or could he? There was that old matter of the morphine poisoning in which Jefferson had said the nurse had been involved; and although the law forbade that a person once acquitted could ever be retried for the same crime, it could not prevent jurors from remembering and being influenced accordingly.

And in any case, had he the right to let matters go that far?

Or would they? Would not the murderer solve the problem for him by coming forward with a confession as soon as the nurse was arrested? This was no ordinary criminal who would be content to sit back and let an innocent person be made to pay for the crime.

For a moment relief surged through him at the thought of this way out of his dilemma; but almost as quickly as it had come, it was gone again. Suppose that Jefferson refused to believe that confession, just as he had refused to believe— And by that time it might be impossible for anyone to produce that one vital piece of evidence that would prove the murderer's guilt.

Stephen glanced at the clock again. Twenty minutes of the half hour were now gone, and it would take nearly all of the remaining ten to drive out to the Heisys'. Although he would almost rather have cut off his right arm, he reached for the telephone and called the Marsden's number.

"Mrs. Marsden, this is Steve Carter," he said a moment later. "Jeff's located Miss Godwin, and he's gone to arrest her for the murders. I'm afraid I'm going to have to tell him the truth."

There was a brief silence at the other end of the wire; then:

"So you know the truth,' the old lady observed slowly. "I might have guessed you would."

"Yes, ma'am," Stephen said, and added sincerely, "I wish I didn't."

"Where is Helen?" Mrs. Marsden asked.

"She's been staying at the Heisy's. I'm about to go out there now."

"I see." There was another brief pause; then: "I'll watch from my window until I see you arrive, Stephen. Then I'll make Ronnie and Whitney take me over there."

Stephen replaced the receiver and left the office just as the first drops of rain began to fall.

17

ELUCIDATION

(Friday, 2:55 p.m. to 3:40 p.m.)

"Repeat for me once more, Miss Godwin, the conversation that took place between you and Ralph Marsden the night he was killed," Jefferson directed. She had already repeated it for him twice, and he knew it practically by heart; but he was playing for time. Stephen still had three minutes.

"But I've already told you everything, Mr. Carter," the nurse protested in weary desperation. "I don't know any more. Honest to God I don't!"

"Look here, Jeff Carter," Miss Maime broke in, twisting her hands nervously in the folds of her skirt. "Are you trying to accuse this girl of anything? Answer me yes or no."

"I'm sorry, Miss Heisy," Jefferson replied with as much patience as he could muster, "but I'm asking questions just now, not answering them. Of course, if you'd prefer it, we can take Miss Godwin down to my office and finish—" He broke off as a peal sounded on the doorbell. "That's Steve!" he exclaimed, springing up in relief. "Never mind, Miss Phoebe; I'll let him in."

He left the room to return a moment later accompanied by Stephen, whose clothes were dripping water.

Miss Phoebe hurried forward solicitously.

"Child, you're soaking wet!" she exclaimed, taking his limp hat. "Don't tell me you walked out here in this storm!"

"No, ma'am," Stephen answered. "I drove, but I forgot to put the top of the car up."

"Im going to get you one of Whitney's coats to put on," she announced, and bustled off.

Stephen glanced around the room, spoke politely to Miss Maime and grinned at the nurse.

"Why, Miss Godwin!" he exclaimed. "Imagine finding you here!" She scowled at him.

"Yes," she mimicked. "Just imagine it! Surprised, aren't you?"

"Cut out the horseplay, Steve," Jefferson interposed, "and get down to business. You've kept us waiting long enough."

Stephen crossed to a chair, attempted to remove Miss Phoebe's knitting from its seat, and succeeded instead in spilling the entire

111

contents upon the floor. He stooped and picked them up again with what seemed to Jefferson like deliberately exasperating slowness; then he went over and placed them upon the ledge of the mantel facing the open double doors into the hall.

"I don't guess you'll have a complete case against anybody, Jeff," he began, standing in front of the mirror over the mantel and toying with one of Miss Phoebe's knitting needles as he talked, "until you can produce two things: first, the motives for the murders"—he touched one finger of his left hand with the knitting needle to check off the point—"and second, the weapon that was used to kill Dr. Richards." He touched another finger with the needle. "Now I think I can tell you the first, and show you where you can find the second, although I'm telling you right now I'm not relishing the job."

He paused as the doorbell rang again. Miss Maime rose to answer it, but Miss Phoebe, who was already in the hall, was ahead of her. A moment later old Mrs. Marsden stumped into the room on her cane. She was followed by Ronnie and Whitney Hamilton.

"All right, Stephen," she said when she had seated herself on the least treacherous of the available chairs; "you can go ahead now."

He turned around from the mirror.

"I was just about to explain," he said, "the chain of circumstances that led up to the death of your grandson, Mrs. Marsden."

He paused to replace the knitting needle in the bag with its companions; then he began again:

"The roots of this crime extend in two directions. The one goes back five years, when a man made a will leaving thirty thousand dollars in trust for his grandson, to be turned over to him only when and if he married with his grandma's consent. Although nobody realized it at the time—Mr. Leland Marsden least of all—murder was making that will.

"The other root goes back just about six months, when a much younger man was accused unjustly of a crime he had not committed, and was defended by the granddaughter of the man who had made the will. But the two didn't join until this second man, who had fallen in love with his defense counsel by this time, came here to live in order to be near her."

He stopped as a particularly loud peal of thunder crashed across the heavens. Miss Maime shuddered and raised her feet a few inches from the floor. Stephen waited until the last reverberations had died away; then he continued:

"However, these two factors probably never would have resulted in murder if another will hadn't been drawn; this time by the widow of the man who had made the first one. In it she left practically her entire fortune to the younger man I just told you about. Her reason for doing this was because she believed he hesitated to ask her granddaughter to marry him for fear of appearing to be a fortune hunter; and she thought that once he found out, not that he was to be her heir, but merely that the granddaughter wasn't, he'd have no more reason for holding back. She even sent her lawyer next door to convey this information indirectly to the people he was staying with, knowing that they'd pass it along to him."

"Stephen," Mrs. Marsden interrupted, "you weren't supposed to tell that."

"I'm sorry, Mrs. Marsden," he said contritely, "but I had to. You'll know why in a minute."

He turned back to the group in general.

"The next morning," he went on, "this will was signed; and although the woman who signed it didn't realize it any more than her husband had in his case, murder had made a second will.

"In the meantime a third factor had come into the situation, which, while it didn't contribute directly to the murder, helped to complicate matters. A trust fund of fifty thousand dollars had been established under the first will for the family doctor. He was to have the interest on the money for medical research, reporting his use of it to the widow; but in case she died or became in any way incapable of looking after her own affairs, the doctor was to receive the lump sum outright, to handle as he pleased.

"Now human nature being what it is, it's not unnatural, I guess, that the doctor should have preferred the lump sum to the interest, especially since, in that case, he wouldn't be beholden to anybody. Se he worked out a plan for making it appear that the widow of his benefactor wasn't right in her mind, and so was incapable of administering the trusteeship; and to help him with his little scheme, he introduced into the house a nurse against whom he held damaging information in another matter."

"That's a lie!" Helen Godwin broke in. "I had nothing to do with that morphine poisoning case, and you can't prove that I had!"

"I'm not trying to, Miss Godwin," Stephen assured her. "All I'm interested in right now is the murder of Ralph Marsden.

"But the doctor had reckoned without taking into account that the nurse might have ambitions of her own," he resumed, addressing the others again. "She hadn't been in the house long before she began, as the saying goes, to set her cap for the grandson. He, for his part, was attracted to her; and besides, he saw in marrying her a chance to get control of the money his grandpa had left for him.

"But there was a little matter of getting his grandma's consent. He wasn't so sure that he could do that; and besides, he'd gotten the idea—a wrong idea, I feel right sure—that his cousin, the granddaughter, would use her influence to prevent it. And then, on the very day that his grandma's will was signed, he all of a sudden hit upon a plan for making his cousin help him.

"He knew or had guessed that the real reason the man who wanted to marry his cousin—and whom she wanted to marry—was holding back was because he felt that he had no right to marry her until the cloud of that other, unsolved crime had been removed from him. Now he had in his possession a letter from this man's dead wife, that would have cleared the whole matter up; so that evening he went to his cousin and told her that he'd give her this letter if she'd promise to use her influence to get their grandma's consent to his marriage to the nurse.

"If he'd stopped there, things might have been all right. But he didn't. Most likely believing that his cousin was to be made their grandma's sole heir, he wanted her to promise to see to it that he received at least half of the estate.

"But it wasn't the idea of the money that made his cousin hesitate to agree to the bargain. He had let her read the letter; and there had been something in it that had showed—

"But I don't guess we need to go into that," he broke off abruptly after a quick glance at Ronnie and Whitney, who were sitting tensely side by side on the sofa. "The point is that the girl couldn't decide whether the knowledge that he could now clear himself of all suspicion of that old crime would compensate to the man for the hurt of knowing what was in that letter; so she took her problem to one of the women with whom the man was staying, in the hope that this woman, who she knew loved him deeply as she did, although in a different way, might be able to help her make the right decision.

"But while they were talking the matter over, the man himself overheard—"

"You don't need to go any further, Steve," Jefferson interrupted. "So it was Hamilton after all!"

He swung upon Whitney.

"You couldn't bear to part with half of that fortune, even to clear your own name, could you, Hamilton?" he demanded. "But you weren't sure that you could get Mrs. Marsden's consent to marry her granddaughter unless you did. You had to have that letter; so you committed one murder to clear yourself of another."

"That's not true!" Ronnie cried, springing up. "Whitney didn't know he was to receive Gram's money. I didn't know it myself until your brother said so a few minutes ago."

"Now keep your shirt on, Jeff," Stephen put in as the district attorney was about to speak again. "Hamilton didn't kill Ralph Marsden; I told you that before. Besides, you ought to realize that he wouldn't have been fool enough to think Mrs. Marsden wouldn't consent to his marrying Miss Ronnie if he knew she was leaving him her money for that very purpose.

"Ralph was killed because of his own greed," he went on, turning back to the group once more. "You see, there was somebody else who didn't want Whitney Hamilton to lose half of that fortune; somebody who had guessed the terms of Mrs. Marsden's will.

"That night, this person decided to try to frighten Ralph into handing over the letter and, seeing the light in his den, called him on his private telephone—which was independent from the main house telephone—to ask to see him in private."

"Hold on a minute, Carter," Whitney interposed. "If you're trying to cast suspicion upon Ronnie, you're crazy. Why should she have bothered to call him up on the telephone, when all she'd have needed to do was walk into the room where he was? And besides, she'd just arranged to buy the damned letter from him for twenty-five thousand dollars. Why should she have—"

"Not so fast, old son," Stephen interrupted him. "I didn't say it was Miss Ronnie who called Ralph up, and I didn't mean to imply that it was. But it was a phone on the Marsdens' line that was used to call him; not in the house, but outside of it. I knew that, because when Mrs. Marsden went to call me at about the same time, she had to wait because the line was in use.

"Oh, I realize that that doesn't prove that the person who was using it was calling Ralph," he went on quickly, as though sensing an objection, "but taken in connection with other things—"

"Wait!" Ronnie broke in excitedly. "You say it was a telephone on our line that was used to call Ralph. But the only other phone on our line is—is—" She broke off and glanced half fearfully at Miss Maime.

"Suppose you let me tell the rest of it, Miss Ronnie, before you start jumping to conclusions," Stephen suggested. "You see, the person who killed your cousin Ralph didn't start out with any such intention at all. All she wanted to do was to frighten him with the revolver, so that he'd give up the letter. But—"

A terrific clap of thunder drowned out his words, while every object in the room assumed for an instant an unearthly quality in the livid flash of lightning which it had accompanied.

"Holy Mother!" Detective Donovan muttered, crossing himself. "That struck somethin' close, as sure as the blessed angels have wings!"

The district attorney was staring about the room as though he had suddenly made a discovery.

"Where's Miss Phoebe?" he demanded.

"Miss Phoebe?" Stephen repeated innocently. "Why, isn't she here? Oh, yes, I recollect now: She said she was going to get me a dry coat to put on. She must have stopped to—"

Miss Maime cut across his words. Her voice was grimly triumphant.

"It's all right, Stephen," she said. "You don't need to beat about the bush any longer. Phoebe drove off in her car over twenty minutes ago, right after she saw you in the looking glass fiddling with that knitting needle, and heard what you said about knowing where the weapon was that killed the doctor,"

18

CONCLUSION

(Friday, 7 p.m. to 7:20 p.m.)

"Don't take it so badly, Steve," Jefferson said that evening. "After all, it wasn't your fault. It was one of those freak accidents that occur only once in about ten thousand. Forbes says there was a spot on her left rear tire where the rubber was worn completely off. That must have acted as a sort of grounding."

They had just learned two hours earlier that the final lightning flash that had climaxed the storm and Stephen's story together had struck Miss Phoebe's little electric coupe, killing her instantly.

"I know," Stephen said miserably. "But if I'd only had the sense to keep my big mouth shut until after the storm was over, she might have gotten away."

But Jefferson shook his head.

"No," he said, "that museum piece of a car would have been spotted and picked up half an hour after the alarm for her had been sent out. She'd have been brought back to stand trial; and she couldn't have done it. The disgrace and strain of it would have killed her before it was half over. It was easier and better this way.

"And by the way," he went on after a slight pause, "Whitney Hamilton called up a little while ago to thank you for giving her that chance. I pretended to be Juniper. After all, I'm supposed to be the district attorney in this county; I couldn't very well let him know I was condoning my own brother's part in aiding a murderer to escape."

Stephen looked up.

"How's he taking it?" he asked.

"He's pretty much broken up over it, naturally," Jefferson replied. "He thought a lot of that little old lady, just as she did of him. But he said he's glad it turned out the way it did. He knows what she'd have had to go through if it hadn't as well as I do—probably even better."

A silence fell after that, which lasted for several minutes. Finally Jefferson broke it.

"And to think," he observed, "that she came into my office the morning after Marsden was shot and actually confessed; and I didn't have the normal intelligence to realize that she was telling the

117

truth! I thought she was doing it to protect Hamilton."

"She was," Stephen affirmed. "And that should have shown us the motive behind the whole thing, Jeff."

"How do you mean?" Jefferson asked, puzzled.

"Because," Stephen explained, "we should have realized that if she thought enough of Whitney Hamilton to confess to a murder to save him, she'd have been willing to commit the murder for his sake in the first place. Not that I think she set out with any such deliberate intention in mind," he added quickly. "I believe it happened just like she told you that morning: She went over there to try to frighten Ralph into giving her Ruth Hamilton's letter, only he didn't scare as easily as she'd expected or he didn't think the gun she had was loaded. And when he tried to take it away from her, it went off and killed him."

"Was that how you knew she'd done it?" Jefferson asked. "The motive, I mean?"

"No," Stephen answered. "Fact is, old Mrs. Marsden saw the truth several hours before I did. I think she got it the minute I told her the Heisys' gun had been used. But it was her insistence that I try to make you drop the whole investigation that put me onto it."

"How was that?" Jefferson asked curiously.

"I knew that she wouldn't have made a request like that without a pretty strong reason," Stephen exclaimed. "Either she'd committed the murder herself or she knew who had. But she hadn't done it, because she was talking to me at the time; I heard the shot over the telephone. It had to be the other reason.

"This afternoon, sort of thinking out loud, I asked Juniper if somebody in his family had been murdered and he wanted the whole thing hushed up, what reason he'd have. He told me that he'd do it if he was right fond of the person who had committed the murder. That gave me my answer."

"I don't see how," Jefferson objected. "That explanation could have applied equally well to Ronnie or even to Whitney Hamilton."

"Sure 'nough," Stephen acknowledged, "but there were other things that I saw the significance of as soon as Juniper's remark had put me on the right track. For instance, there was Miss Maime Heisy's sudden stop as she was about to tell us what she said to Miss Phoebe when she saw that man leaving the Marsdens' that night. That showed me that Miss Phoebe wasn't there to say anything to, and Miss Maime had just remembered it. And Miss Phoebe herself didn't mention having seen any man, although she would have if she'd been there, since, according to Miss Maime, they shared the same bedroom.

"Then Miss Phoebe was the only person who knew both that Whitney Hamilton was to be Mrs. Marsden's heir, and that Ralph Marsden had that letter. That made her the only person with a reason for not wanting Ronnie to consent to Ralph's terms."

"But I thought," Jefferson put it slyly, "that you didn't tell the Heisys that Hamilton was to receive Mrs. Marsden's money, but only that Ronnie wasn't."

Stephen smiled reminiscently.

"Jeff," he said, "you've known the Heisys a lot longer than I have. You ought to realize that you only need to tell them half of a thing, and they'll smell out the other half by instinct."

"Yes, I guess you're right about that," Jefferson admitted with a grin. He was remembering a certain remark of Miss Phoebe's.

"Finally," Stephen concluded, "there was that business about the telephones. Miss Maime had told me that their phone was on the same line as the Marsdens'; and Mrs. Marsden had told me that night when she called up that she hadn't been able to call right away, because her line was busy. Now we know from what the nurse told us that somebody had called Ralph that night around two o'clock, although you weren't inclined to put much stock in that at the time. But if she was telling the truth, it wasn't unnatural to suppose that Ralph's telephone and one on his grandma's line had been connected. I don't guess the Heisys are in the habit of making many calls in the middle of the night; and in view of the other things I've just pointed out, it looked like it must have been Miss Phoebe who was calling Ralph."

"I see," Jefferson said. "And besides, all that fitted in exactly with the story she told that morning when she made her confession."

He lighted a cigar and took one or two thoughtful puffs. Then he asked:

"But why did she kill Richards, Steve? I gathered from what happened this afternoon that she must have stabbed him with one of those steel knitting needles you made a point of diddling with in front of the mirror when you talked about the weapon; but what made her do it?"

"I guess you might call it self-defense," Stephen replied. "She was willing to sacrifice herself to save Whitney Hamilton if need be, but she was not willing to be sacrificed by the doctor to no purpose, now that you had admitted to her that there wasn't enough evidence for you to arrest Hamilton. She wanted to go on living if she could; and she wasn't sure that she could with Richards knowing what he did."

"You mean," Jefferson asked, "that Richards knew she had shot Ralph Marsden?"

"He must have," Stephen replied. "Or anyway, he guessed it after he'd talked to her. The fact that he jumped to the conclusion that she was the one who had seen him, in preference to Miss Maime, shows that he must have seen and recognized her somewhere about the grounds of one of the two houses, although I don't guess it ever occurred to him at the time that she had shot Ralph, or he wouldn't have sent for her to make a bid for her silence.

"I guess we can figure out pretty well what must have happened there in the office, Jeff. When she told him that it wasn't she, but her sister, who had seen him, he all of a sudden realized what her own presence there had meant. He realized too not only that he had nothing to fear from her, but that he could actually prove his own innocence, if the need arose, by turning her over to the police. Pleased with himself and his sudden mastery of the situation, he must have thrown back his head and laughed in her face. And poor Miss Phoebe, driven to desperation and seeing his exposed throat . . ."

"You're probably right," Jefferson agreed. "Lord, Steve! It looks as though neither one of us has been very bright in the handling of this case. Why, she actually told us that no one could have gone in and killed Richards after she left, and we never got the significance of it."

He took another puff at his cigar; then he observed soberly:

"It's funny, though, how things turn out. Here nature's meted out to her the identical punishment that the state would have demanded: death by electrocution."

Stephen nodded.

"Except," he amended, "that nature did it more quickly and more mercifully. She probably never even knew what had happened. I don't guess, Jeff, that I'm sorry about how it turned out after all."

www.ingramcontent.com/pod-product-compliance
Lightning Source LLC
Chambersburg PA
CBHW050803250626
47155CB00005B/2185